Death by Sugar
A Jesse Clarke Mystery
Helen Goltz

Atlas Productions

Death by Sugar

First published in 2010. Reprinted 2015 and 2025.

Cover art: Art by Karri – https://www.artbykarri.com/

Proofreading by Ro Parkinson

Please note:

In my books, no animals, including Jesse's beloved boxer, Atlas, ever get harmed, dog-napped, threatened, injured or die. So rest easy, dear reader, and read on in peace.

I proudly support the WSPA (World Society for the Protection of Animals) and Animals Australia. I thank them for their continued efforts to make the world kinder to animals.

This book is written in British/Australian English.

Chapter 1

I WAS SAVOURING A skinny cappuccino and admiring the black Mercedes parked across the road when it blew up. That doesn't usually happen. Most cars I admire continue in one piece.

It was Sunday, and being a creature of habit, Atlas the Boxer and I slept in until around 9am. It is known in our household, which consists of just Atlas and me, as no-alarm clock Sunday. Saturday is also known as no-alarm clock, but that was yesterday and irrelevant to the car bombing. This morning, we rose right at 9am and went for our jog. Atlas pulled for the first twenty minutes, and then I pulled him home for the last ten minutes. I followed this with a selection of weights designed to keep me looking young, lithe and beautiful; two out of three ain't bad, and then, after a shower, feeling tingly in mind and body and with a happy dog snoozing on the front deck, I walked down to my local café society and ordered scrambled eggs on toast, no butter, and a skinny cappuccino.

I read their Sunday newspaper—it's too trashy for me to buy—and watched the regulars and new faces come and go.

When he's not running classes, Dominic will join me. If I'm really disciplined, I'll join one of Dom's classes! But that requires getting up at 6.30am on a weekend and sweating with other people. This was one weekend Dom went alone. He was running back-to-back classes, but he was working on joining me for the second round of coffee.

I continued sipping my skinny cappuccino, watching the panic unfold outside the café. The owner, who wasn't in the car when it blew up, was having a lucky day in my opinion. He didn't seem to think so. He was a good-looking man, tall, dark, with an in-vogue stubble on his face. His blue jeans, leather jacket, black t-shirt and scarf wrapped around his neck gave him a bohemian look. He paced around the car and watched it burn, his hands moving from his hips to his head. The emergency service sirens wailing towards us seemed to perk him up. An ambulance arrived first, no doubt to treat a portly, middle-aged woman who paced and hyperventilated behind the driver. She wasn't injured but kept repeating that it could have been her, unlikely, unless she was going to self-combust. I suspected she meant she could have been hurt. My detecting skills were improving even though I had only had two clients so far.

My publicity skills, however, were much sharper after fifteen years of practice. I figured this was a case of 'all publicity is good publicity' for the café. The news crew arrived before the emergency service crew and did a fine job filming the burning car with the café logo in the background. I wondered if it would deter people from coming here again or encourage them; the place to be on a Sunday morning!

I spotted Dominic. Tall and dark, buffed and radiant after a full morning's workout. He crossed the road, his vision fixated on the car. He pushed open the glass door of the cafe and entered, dropped into the seat next to me and kissed me without taking his eyes off the car.

'Mercedes SLK55 AMG roadster convertible!'

'Very well, thanks!' I answered.

He looked at me and grinned. 'Is this your fault?'

'Hmm, probably.'

'What happened?'

I shrugged. 'It just blew up.' I clicked my fingers. 'Like that!'

'Wow, really?' He grabbed the menu and scanned it. Dominic had the same breakfast every time. The waiter arrived, and he ordered the full breakfast with a flat white and another coffee for me.

'I'm starving. After we eat, do you want to go home, and you know what?' he looked at me.

'What?' I asked without thinking.

'Do it!' he whispered. 'We could go back to my place after we eat and ...'

'I love your directness,' I cut him off. 'I'm surprised you have enough energy after two gym classes.'

Dominic shrugged. 'It gets my adrenalin racing.'

'Come to think of it, we had our first date after one of your gym classes,' I recalled.

'I know. I was thinking about doing it then, too,' Dominic poured a glass of water.

'In that order – eat then sex?'

'God, no.'

'See, familiarity breeds contempt. Now that we've become regular, you want to eat first. This is why I don't think we should move in together ... soon you'll want to eat and nothing else,' I teased him.

'Trust me,' he moved closer, putting his hand on my leg, 'I'd scrap breakfast in a flash to go home and ...' he decided not to finish his sentence. 'Change the subject, or I'll need a cold shower.' He pulled off his navy sweater and ran his hand through his hair. Frowning, he looked out the window again. I followed his gaze, and we watched as the police arrived. They moved people away from the car, cordoning off the area. A young officer flipped pages in his notebook and then started to take a statement from the driver.

'What happened?' Dominic asked.

'Well, I got here at about 10.15, and at about 10.25, that car pulled into the car space. The driver got out, came in here, ordered a long black, and sat in that window seat. Ten minutes later, his phone rang. He went outside to talk and walked towards his car. Before he crossed the road, the car blew up. He dropped the phone and ran to the car, but there was a lot of heat in the air so he ran back again. The staff called the police and fire brigade. I don't know who called the ambulance. He's been pacing around ever since. No one came near his car the whole time.'

I turned back to find Dominic grinning at me.

'You're getting good at this, Ms Clarke!'

'That's Detective Clarke to you, buddy.'

'How many cases do you have to get before you can afford to give up your publicity business?'

I shrugged. 'I don't know that I want to give it up. I could just pick and choose one or two clients at a time and juggle them with the PI stuff. Quality of life, you know.'

'I wish. Ed can handle the publicity business, can't he?' he referred to my business partner.

'Ed just wants to manage a few clients at a time. Then he can head off early each day for his pilates class!'

Dominic laughed. 'Can't picture big Ed doing pilates.'

'Simon is into it ... the things we do for love.'

'Can't picture big Ed with a boyfriend.'

'The hair's a bit of a giveaway.' I thought about Ed's dedication to his hair. 'When a guy spends more time than a girl in the bathroom, it's a fair bet he may bat for the other side.'

Dominic nodded his agreement.

'Why don't you go and give this guy your business card? He may need a PI to find who blew up his pride and joy.'

I frowned. 'I'm not good at self-promotion. Besides, I've only had one case since qualifying ... I'm not confident yet. I'd rather the clients walked in the door.'

'I'll give it to him.' Dominic jumped up and was gone before I could protest. I watched him walk up to the guy and make small talk about the car. They were matched in height, and both stood, arms crossed, looking at the vehicle. Eventually, the police officer returned to talk to the driver. Dominic offered my card, the guy pocketed it, they shook hands and Dominic returned.

He slid into the seat beside me.

'What did he say?' I asked him.

'Nothing sensible. He's a bit shocked and probably won't look at the card until later. He's just waiting for the fire brigade and tow truck now.'

I leaned towards him and kissed his cheek. 'Thank you, Dom!'

'Detecting is us!' he smiled. 'Got any handcuffs?'

'Do you really want to go there again?'

'Maybe,' he leaned back as the waiter delivered his breakfast and the coffees. He wasted no time starting.

Outside, the fire truck's siren could be heard wailing towards us as people scattered out of the way.

Chapter 2

I saw the driver of the Mercedes before he saw me. I just happened to be standing at my office window at the time when, down below, I saw him arrive on a motorcycle. He took the helmet off, stood on the street outside my office building and looked down at my business card. He looked towards the third floor before taking the half-dozen stairs to the front door and into the foyer. He was dressed in black pants and a black leather jacket. His hair was tied back in a short ponytail.

I heard the lift arrive, but there was no sign of him yet. If you knew where you were going, it would have taken about 13 seconds to get from the lift to our office. I've timed it. I assumed he was looking at the card again or fixing his hair, but it was probably the former. Eventually, he arrived in my office's doorway. He looked around, confused. There were no markings on it for a publicity or PI business.

I stood and went towards the reception desk in front of my desk and to the right of Ed's. Behind both of our desks was a boardroom for meetings with clients.

'Hello, Jesse Clarke,' I extended my hand.

'Right,' he looked down at the card, then shook my hand firmly. 'I met a guy yesterday. He gave me this card. I thought he was Jesse Clarke.'

'Could go either way, I guess. But no, that was ... um ... he promotes the business.'

'Right,' he said agai,n pocketing the card and looking at me. 'You're short for a PI.'

'Yeah,' I agreed. 'The manual said five foot eight, but with heels on, I just qualified.'

He looked at me, unsure. My wit was wasted on him; Ed would have laughed if he had been in the office. I pointed to a seat; the boardroom didn't seem necessary. I watched as he sat down with trepidation. I hoped we would get down to business before Ed came back. Ed's new blonde streaks may scare him off. He removed his leather jacket. Underneath, he wore a long black fitted shirt. He looked good. I had always been good at detecting handsome men. It was a skill that came naturally.

'And you are?'

'Ah, yea,h right, sorry. Renzo Leonardo. Call me Ren.'

'You're the owner of the sports car, the one that blew up yesterday.'

'Yeah, a Mercedes SLK55 AMG roadster convertible.'

'So I heard.' I waited, he said nothing.

I continued. 'Are you from the Leonardo family which owns the Italian restaurant *Leonardo's*?

'Yeah, been there?' his eyes lit up.

'Sure. It's great.'

'Thanks. It's been in the family for a long time; I'm managing it now. Been thinking of changing the name to the Italian Stallion,' he shrugged. 'What do you think?'

I tried not to groan. 'Risky, you've got such a strong brand name; be a shame to ruin all those years of goodwill.'

'Yeah, I was thinking that too. Come down some time; I'll make sure you are looked after. Bring a friend.'

'Love to, thanks. So can I get you a tea or coffee?'

'No, I'm good, thanks,' Ren answered.

I waited again. Nothing. 'So you want me to find who blew it up?'

'Can you do that?'

'I'll give it a fair go.'

'Can I afford you?'

'I'm not cheap,' I smiled at him. Again, wasted wit. I mentioned my rates, and he nodded. I didn't detect any panic.

'OK. Well, how does this work? Will you call me?' he rose.

'Well, I need to talk to you for a bit first, and then I'll get to work on it, and I'll call you every few days or once a week with an update, whatever you prefer.'

'Will you be talking to the cops as well?'

'Yes. Did you want to talk to me now?'

'Can't now. I've got to get to work.'

'OK, we can do it later. So you're riding the bike now?'

'Yeah, I've got another Merc, but I'm a bit nervous about that now. Why? Do you think the bike's at risk too?'

'No ... maybe ... I don't know, I was just curious,' I nodded towards the leather jacket. 'A stable of vehicles, huh?' I wondered if he'd make the link: stallion – stable, vehicles ... never mind.

'It's my thing,' he shrugged, 'I collect things I like.'

I nodded; it sounded creepy, and I could think of a lot of questions about that statement. 'Can we meet tomorrow?'

We agreed to meet at his restaurant before it opened for business. He rose, and I walked him out.

Client number two. The business was booming!

'Do I get a cut, like a commission, for bringing in business?' Dominic asked as he perched on the edge of my desk.

'Only fair, I think,' Ed agreed.

I looked from one to the other. I began, 'Ed, tell me, when Dom started his personal trainer business, and we did the publicity for him, did we ever get paid for that job?'

Ed grinned. 'I think I sent the invoice, but I remember the client saying he would pay in kind.'

'And I have!' Dominic stated. 'Many, many times and still, I'm willing to go on paying in kind.'

'What a guy!' I smiled at him.

'I resent and resemble that remark,' he teased and slid off the desk. 'Let's go; it's after five. Ed, haven't you got a pilates class to go to or something?'

'Not tonight. Tonight is brisk walk and martinis night.'

'One counteracts the other,' Dominic frowned.

'It does, but I walk fast to earn that martini. What have you two love birds got planned?'

'Tonight is good sex and beer night,' Dominic looked hopeful.

'Is it?' I played him. 'I thought it was Sav Blanc and Dom cooks night!'

Ren's restaurant was in the main precinct of the west end, huddled among shops and cafes with similar dark timber facades that spoke of hard work, eccentric characters, and tales to tell. Further up the street, progress had moved in. A contemporary cement block of units in bright colours looked out of place, and a row of glass boutiques offering permanent sales of clothing and shoes encroached on the village feel. Much was written about the area and the battle by locals to fight off developers and progress.

Three senior Italian men sat at the front of the restaurant on a timber bus seat. Their faces were worn, they puffed on small stubs of cigarettes, and there was considerable hand waving as they spoke. I loved the character of the area, but I stood out like an alien who wanted to belong but was more suited to the collared units and glass shops.

I pushed open the door to Ren's restaurant and entered. It had a rich ambience, warm brown and burgundy colours, plush booths, dark timber tables, and lamps. On a beautiful sunny day, it might feel claustrophobic, but given the wind chill and grey skies, it was inviting. My eyes adjusted to the dim lighting, and I spotted Ren behind the bar. He waved and came over. We slipped into a booth, and he beckoned one of his staff. I asked for an English Breakfast Tea.

Ren wore jeans and another black shirt. I guessed his wardrobe was predominantly black.

'I rang the cops this morning,' he frowned. 'They're clueless.'

I shrugged. 'They've got a stack of work on and I imagine the fire has ruined any evidence that may have been in the car.'

I got the contact details of the officer he had been dealing with before continuing.

'Do you think someone tried to kill me or was just trying to scare me to death?' he asked.

'I don't know. You're still alive, so that's a positive sign,' I assured him.

'So how are you going to solve it?'

'Good question.' I tried to conceal my panic, and the words *How the hell do I know* threatened to slip out. 'I'm going to start by asking lots of questions, finding some facts, putting it all together, and seeing if it directs us somewhere.'

'OK, shoot.' He leaned across the table and glared at me as though preparing for a round of *Who Wants to be a Millionaire*.

'I'll be asking questions of other people too, not just you.'

'Oh, sure,' he relaxed; now he wasn't responsible for carrying the whole case on his shoulders. His expression changed. 'Like who?'

'It'll depend on where each of the leads ... uh ... leads me. I may need to talk to the cops, your insurance company, your mechanic, witnesses at the coffee shop, that kind of thing.'

'Fine. Just make sure they know you're working for me. I don't want them to think I'm being investigated.'

'I understand,' I assured him. 'So, do you have any natural enemies?' I began.

'What do you mean?'

'Well, you know, seals are natural enemies for turtles, dogs for cats, birds for worms, that kind of thing ...' He looked lost. 'Do you know anyone who would want to blow up your car?'

'Shit, yeah. Who wouldn't want to blow it up? If you saw a guy driving a sleek, black Mercedes roadster convertible, wouldn't you want to rough him or the car up?'

'No.'

He shrugged. 'I would. It's like the haves and have-nots. People check me out and think, 'How did that guy get that? What kind of business is he in? Let's get him'.'

I nodded. I was going to need a stronger drink than tea. 'So?'

'What?' He asked.

I reiterated the question.

'Not off the top of my head,' he answered, 'like I don't have any enemies if that's what you mean?'

'That's what I mean.' *Rich and stupid*, I thought. I made a mental note to ask short and direct questions.

'Tell me exactly what you did that morning from when you got up until your car was blown up,' I instructed. I opened my pad and waited, pen at the ready. I thought that looked professional; at least my publicity clients liked to see me taking notes.

He thought for a few seconds. 'I got up, had a shave and a dump ... '

I winced; my fault for saying 'exactly'.

'... got in the shower, then got dressed. I checked on Vince – he's my best friend, staying with me for a while – he was out of it, so I got in the car and got a coffee. I parked the car, went into the coffee joint and went straight to the front counter. I ordered a coffee, drank it and then the phone rang, so I answered it, but I couldn't hear who it was, so I went outside to see if the reception was better and as I walked towards my car, it blew up. Jeez, if I hadn't taken that call, I could be history now.'

He looked at me, finished. I hadn't made any notes. I sighed and started from the beginning, breaking down each thing he did, except for the 'dump', and worked him through it in detail. Fifty minutes later, he looked glazed over, so I let him go. The publicity business was starting to look good again.

Chapter 3

'HAVE YOU HEARD OF Elizabeth J. Rowan?' Ed accosted me as I walked back into the office after interviewing the Italian Stallion. The windows were open, and the air conditioning was off – being able to open the windows was one of the benefits of being in an old building – and Ed liked to breathe fresh air.

'Did she write the *Harry Potter* books?' I asked.

'No, that's J.K. Rowling. Not even close.'

'OK, I give up, who's Elizabeth J. Rowan?'

'Our new publicity client!' Ed announced. 'She came by while you were out. I told her I would have to check it by you, but I was fairly confident we could handle her work.'

'We're finishing up the film and the play this wee,k aren't we?' I asked.

'Yes and we have two more weeks to run on the water conservation campaign. We can handle it.'

'I'm happy for you to make those decisions, Ed. You don't have to consult me. We've worked together long enough to know if it's right for the agency.'

'I'm touched,' he placed his hand on his heart. 'Anyway, she's an artist.'

'Really?'

'Well, she thinks she is. Her *Memories of Summer* exhibition opens the first week of autumn at the Gallery. She wants us to handle the publicity.'

'Sounds charming.' I boiled the kettle and raised a cup to Ed. He nodded. I measured the instant coffee into two cups. '*Memories of Summer*. I still remember summer clearly.'

'That's because it's still summer,' Ed reminded me. 'But it won't be when the exhibition opens.'

'Oh, right, makes sense ... no need to see the exhibition right now, just look out the window! Is she reasonable talent?' I asked.

'She can string a sentence together; she'll be OK on the radio.'

'And TV and print?'

'Well, she's no glamour puss, but not frightening either.'

Ed had a way with words, which is why he was one of the best publicists around and why I hired him to join my business.

'What did you quote her?'

'Our middle-of-the-road rate. She looked a bit hungry.'

'That's fine. Here's to summer!' I handed him his coffee and sat down at my desk. 'Any messages?'

'Dom rang. What a shame he isn't gay,' Ed sighed.

'A real waste,' I agreed.

'I told him you were seeing a client. So, got any leads?'

'Indeed,' I pulled out my notes from Renzo Leonardo. 'I'm going to start with the roommate, Vince Palino.'

'Brilliant deduction, Watson!' Ed grinned.

'You know, my mother's maiden name was Watson,' I said.

'See, it's in the blood!' Ed exclaimed.

❧

I pushed the buzzer on apartment six and waited. *So this is where Ren, the Italian Stallion, lives. Nice.*

'Yeah?' a male voice came through the intercom.

'Hi, Jesse Clarke to speak with Vince Palino.'

'Yeah, come on up. Second floor, apartment six.'

I heard the buzzer and pulled open the front door. It was a beautiful apartment block on the outside—old-world façade and great fretwork—but the inside was just as up-market. My heels clicked on the marble floor. I stopped and thought about what I was doing.

Should I go up alone? I should have asked this guy to meet me in a public place.

I rang Ed and told him the address. He offered to come over, but instead, we agreed he would call my phone in fifteen minutes.

How much damage could Vince do in fifteen minutes? Images of *Law and Order* chalk outlines raced through my head. *I needed to be more careful if I was going to continue in this line of business.*

I arrived outside the apartment, and before my knuckles touched the door, it opened. An unshaven, overweight and balding man checked me out.

'Jesse?' he asked.

'Yes. Vince?'

'Yeah, come on in.'

He moved aside, and I entered. Vince needed a hose down. He looked like he hadn't shaved for a few days and smelt like a bottle of scotch. The apartment, on the other hand, was pristine; you could eat off the floor; it was so clean. It was modern and a contradiction to the façade.

I thought about Renzo. His unit was a complete contrast to his workplace. The unit had an unlived-in feel, as if Ren had bought a display unit and just put his clothes in the cupboard. Everything was white tiles, cream rugs and mirror tiles – too many mirror tiles. There was a reasonable view of the park square and district views on all sides. The cream curtains were necessary for privacy at night, given the proximity of the units next door. I wondered if Ren cared or was happy to be on show in his glass house; he was a bit of a peacock.

Vince looked out of place as if he should have been in the garage. I wanted to get a cloth and run behind him, wiping off his fingerprints, but I got over that.

'Nice place,' I said for want of a conversation starter.

'Yeah, Ren likes to keep it neat for the ladies. Says they appreciate that.'

'We do,' I nodded.

'Not that he's ever cleaned a day in his life.' Vince dropped down on the couch. I took that as a clear sign tea or coffee would not be forthcoming.

Vince continued. 'Ren's mother cleans nearly every second day and does his washing and ironing.'

I had a new picture of Renzo in my mind now. He'd become less of an Italian stallion and more of a foal!

Vince folded his arms across his chest; his stomach, barely encased in a grey buttoned-down shirt, protruded below his arms. He gave the impression that he wouldn't be outsmarted by anyone, least of all a female PI. Within the first ten minutes of our meeting, he told me that he had bought all his clothes in Europe, was passionate about sports cars, and was linked to the right people if I needed anything. Handy! It appeared to be important to him to impress me. He sat back, spread out his hairy arms on the back of the white leather lounge and showed more stomach as it tugged on his buttoned shirt – way too much hair on display. Vince and Ren were like chalk and cheese. It must be hard to play second fiddle to a best friend who would always catch the girls' eye first. *Hmm, motive?*

'So what do you want to know?' Vince put his feet up on the frosted glass coffee table.

Size 10 runners. I stored the detail away … you never know. I was getting good at this.

'How long have you known Ren?'

'Since we were in the womb! Our mothers were pregnant at the same time. We went to the same primary school, high school, scout group, soccer club, you name it.'

'How come you're staying here?' I asked.

'Broke up with my girlfriend and moved out. This is just temporary until she takes me back.'

'She'll come to her senses,' I agreed.

'You single?'

'No.' I nipped that in the bud. Besides, I ask the questions here. I continued. 'Do you know of anyone who would want to threaten Ren?'

Vince looked up at the ceiling while he was thinking. He took his time. Eventually, I looked up at the ceiling to ensure he hadn't become distracted by a ceiling mural.

'Nuh. Can't think of anyone,' he answered.

Well, that was worth the wait!

'What about at his work; has his restaurant put anyone out of business, or do you know if they've dropped a long-term supplier, that kind of thing?'

'Nuh, not that he's mentioned to me.'

'Could he have aggravated an ex-girlfriend?' I persisted.

'Nuh.'

'Ex-boyfriend?'

'Nuh.'

'Partner of an ex-girlfriend?'

'Nuh.'

'Business partner?'

'Nuh.'

'Enemy of his father?'

'Nuh.'

'Family enemies like the Capulets and Montagues?'

'Who?'

'You know, like Romeo and Juliette.'

'Never saw it. Nuh.'

'Loan shark?'

'Nuh.'

Vince was a wealth of information.

'Who else does he hang out with?'

'Besides me,' Vince thought again. 'There's Benny. He and Ren are pretty tight.'

'What's Benny's story?'

'He's alright. Married, a stack of kids.'

'How did Benny meet Ren?'

'College, I think. They both did hospitality management or something like that.'

'Anyone else?'

'He's got a few buddies he plays soccer with, and Ren has a different girlfriend every week. He's like a magnet.'

'I'm sure.'

'You know, you look a bit like my girlfriend, uh, ex, same sort of hair.'

'Yeah?' I tried to sound pleased.

'Yeah. She's a looker.'

'Well, thanks.' I hoped I never saw her. I would be unimpressed if she weren't! 'Uh, what's your girlfriend's name and number?'

Vince looked at me with surprise written all over his face.

'Why? Do you think she's involved? How could she be involved?' he smirked.

'I'm not saying she blew up the car ... but stranger things have happened,' I said aloud when I meant to think it to myself. 'I wouldn't mind speaking with her because she's probably observed Ren around you and may have a different take on everything.'

He shrugged. 'I guess.' He rattled off her name and number.

'You can tell her I'm doing just fine and not even thinking about her,' Vince added.

'I'll be sure to,' I assured him.

My phone rang. *Bless you, Ed.*

'Listen, I've got to take this, so thanks for your time; I appreciate it. I'll see myself out.' I was at the door before I had finished the sentence; I would have been in the car if I could have moved quicker in my heels.

'No problem. Might see you again, hey?' He said at the door. 'Ren got your number ... in case I think of anything?'

'He sure has,' I smiled, hoping he didn't call. I reached the elevator and answered the phone.

On the way down, I reviewed what I got from Vince. Nothing!

Chapter 4

'I CAN'T TALK UNTIL I have a drink before me!' My best friend, Melanie Davies, sat back and folded her arms. Her blonde hair was tied back, and her red linen suit was crushed from a day at the office wading over financial statements for clients. Melanie always had a touch of the theatrics about her.

'What, not a word?' I teased.

'OK, I guess I can fill you in on my love life until the vodka arrives. It's non-existent! Here's my drink!' She barely waited for the waiter to place it on the table before raising the glass, inhaling it and taking a sip. She sat back.

'That's better. You're looking good,' she noticed I was there.

'I darkened my hair.'

'It makes your eyes look bluer. Does Dom like it?'

'Don't be silly, he hasn't even noticed.'

'Men. Speaking of which, why are we here?' Melanie glanced around. 'Not that I'm complaining, I like Italian food.'

'Research,' I told her.

'Italian cooking or Italian men?'

'Good grief, don't you think of anything else besides eating and men?'

'Of course. There's shopping.'

'Work research,' I steered her back on track. 'The owner is a new client.'

'Really? This joint's been here for ages. Why have they decided to do some marketing now?'

'No, he's hired a private investigator!'

'Who?'

'Me! Mel, get with the program. He's hired me to investigate a matter for him.'

'Oh!' Her eyes widened. 'Sorry, I'm scatty this evening. Let's start again. So what's he got you investigating, is he good looking and does Dom know?'

'His car blew up, yes and yes.'

She nodded. I could see she was thinking back through her questions.

'What sort of car?'

'Mercedes.' I couldn't remember the model and didn't think Melanie would care anyway.

'Nice. What model?' she asked.

I frowned at her. 'I don't know ... some sort of convertible. It was black.'

'Mm, I like silver better for a convertible. How did he find you?'

'We were there when it blew up. Dom gave him my card.'

'Ah, so Dom's seen him. Well, best you introduce me; I can be like an insider.'

'If you get inside,' I said.

She smiled at me. 'Is that a challenge?'

When I arrived home after my Italian dinner, Dominic was asleep on the couch, and Atlas, the wonder dog, was beside him. The television was on, and neither of them heard me enter. It was good to know they were both alert to intruders; I made a mental note to increase my contents insurance.

Dom didn't sleep over on a Tuesday night because of classes at 6am the next morning. I wondered if he was a little insecure or checking up that I didn't bring the stallion home with me. I watched him for a few minutes; he was too big for the couch and had an extra foot or two of body extended over the side. Atlas, who wasn't allowed on the couch, had managed to worm his way up there and find a comfortable spot behind Dom. The football was playing, and Dom had been channel surfing; the remote was still in his hands. In a wild show of affection, Atlas looked up and wagged his tail, yawned and went back to sleep. I decided to let Dom sleep there until after I had showered and washed my make-up off.

Ten minutes later, I stood under the hot water, washing my hair and thinking about my case. I loved saying that; the novelty would wear off soon enough. What did I know? I knew that Ren had no enemies that he knew of, the family business was secure, he wasn't seeing anyone's wife and he was an avid collector. I was still yet to explore the true meaning of that. He was wealthy, a mommy's boy and had several best buddies, including Vince and Benny. He played soccer; I was yet to investigate that one. He received a call just before the car exploded that he attributes to saving his life, but his life may never have been in danger.

I closed my eyes and rinsed the conditioner from my hair. I had to talk to the police. I needed to know where the bomb was planted and how it was triggered. The thought made me shiver. Much scarier than publicity!

Something touched me, and I squealed and jumped – a spider? No, it was just Dom, naked. He moved into the shower next to me, drawing me closer with his hands around my waist.

'Why didn't you wake me?' he frowned.

'You two boys looked so comfortable.'

He moved his head from side to side. 'You need a bigger couch; it's given me a crick in my neck. If we move in together, I've got a huge couch.'

'You have another huge asset too that I'm particularly interested in,' I teased.

The police station was impressive, brand new, and clean. Even the crims looked better in these surroundings. I made my way to the front desk and asked for Officer Jason Abingdon. We spoke earlier by phone, and he was expecting me. Eventually, he appeared. He was a good-looking, tanned, compact man, about five foot eleven and built of solid muscle. His hair was shaved to stubble all over his head; it made him look tougher. His eyes were a light blue. He invited me into a small interview room. It was clinically clean.

'Nice building.'

'Yeah, we've only been here two months. Give it another six months, and it'll look as bad as the others.' He smiled and showed off a good set of white, straight teeth, the product of braces somewhere along the line. I wondered if his parents hoped those teeth would be engaged somewhere other than on police duties.

'Renzo Leonardo,' he said, opening the file.

'Ren to his friends!' I added. The uniform was making me nervous.

'Yeah, our pal, Ren,' he smiled again. 'OK, what can I tell you? The car's been burnt to a cinder. Nice car, too. Mercedes SLK55 Roadster ...'

'Uh-huh, I know.'

Officer Abingdon continued. 'It contained a homemade explosive consisting of ammonium nitrate fertiliser and sugar.'

'Really, sugar! It always seemed such a friendly substance.'

He laughed. My jokes worked much better on Officer Abingdon than Ren the Italian Stallion.

'So, is it normal to use sugar in a bomb?' I asked.

'I don't know. You may have to speak to a bomb expert.'

'How was it exploded?' I asked.

'We don't know. It could have been a commercial or military explosive, such as semtex.'

'But do you know how it was triggered? He wasn't near the car, so he didn't start the engine or open the door.'

'We don't know that either.'

'Any theories?'

'Sure ... it could have been set off by someone sitting nearby who pushed a trigger when they saw him coming ...'

'That would suggest that they never meant to kill him, just scare him.'

'It would,' Officer Abingdon agreed. 'Or it could have been timed so that it went off at a particular time whether he was in the vehicle or not.'

'If that's the case, it was definitely his lucky day,' I added.

'You can say that again. Or it could have been set off by something like his phone.'

'Really?' I sat forward, my interest sparked. 'He received a call on his way back to the car.'

'Did he say who it was from?'

'No. The car blew up, and that was kind of distracting.' I grabbed my pad and pen and made a note. 'The phone as a trigger, who would have thought?'

'Modern technology, it'll be the end of us all,' Officer Abingdon shook his head.

'Do you know a bomb expert I could talk to?' I asked.

'I can give you a few names from our bomb squad. See if they can help,' he grabbed a piece of paper and opened a black folder that sat next to the phone. He jotted down a few names. 'You can tell them that I sent you, and if you find anything, can you keep me in the loop?'

'Sure, and vice versa, please. While I'm pushing my luck, is there any chance you could run a search on a guy called Vince Palino? He's one of Renzo's best friends and is staying with him at the moment.'

'Do you think he's involved?'

'Wouldn't have a clue.'

Officer Abingdon laughed.

I continued. 'I just wanted to eliminate him.'

'Yeah, I can do that,' he agreed. 'It'll cost you a coffee, though.'

I smiled. 'Small price to pay!' I think Officer Abingdon was hitting on me. This could come in handy. 'So, nothing else in there that could help?' I nodded at the file.

'No.' He pulled out the photos of the car in flames. 'We pretty much told you what we told Renzo. I'd say Renzo's annoyed someone big time.'

***

'Know any bomb experts?' I asked Ed as I dropped my handbag behind the desk and threw Renzo's file into the in-tray.

'Gee, let me think ... no!'

'Do you want to think for a little longer, see if someone comes to mind?' I teased him.

'OK,' he agreed. I watched as he turned his blonde head, with every hair perfectly in place, skywards. Within a second, he turned to look at me. 'No! I don't know any. However, I do know an artist. Elizabeth is due here for a meeting in fifteen minutes to discuss her gallery launch. So glad you could make it in time.'

I frowned. 'Can't you handle Ms Summer and her memories?'

He grinned. 'Yes. But at least she gets to meet you. Otherwise, she'll think I'm just making you up.'

'Have you seen the works in question?'

'Yes,' Ed answered without enthusiasm.

'Right. I take it you won't be buying a piece from the *Memories of Summer* collection?'

'No,' he dropped his voice. 'You might say I'm more of a winter man.'

We heard the elevator stopping at our floor, and we did our best to look busy. We didn't want the clients to think we sat around all day drinking diet cola and pontificating on clients, even though that was pretty much what we did.

I felt a rush of air as Elizabeth whirled in. Ed rose to meet her, and I followed. I was expecting a bohemian artist, but she was just the opposite: about thirty-five and manicured within an inch of her life. The nails were red and perfect, her hair was sprayed and not moving, the make-up was dramatic, and she wore a chiffon dress that looked like she should be waltzing with Ed. The heels were also too high to be sensible. That meant her underwear was also probably not sensible. But she was an artist, although I suspect she was more interested in being a starlet.

'I am so thrilled to meet you and thrilled that you are going to publicise my event. I feel *Memories of Summer* is my best work to date,' Elizabeth gushed.

'That will make our job easy,' I smiled, 'Ed was just saying how truly impressive it was.'

'Oh, you!' She hit his arm.

'I'll make some coffee. You two head to the board room and get started,' I offered.

'Let's do that, Ed,' she lowered her voice and winked at Ed.

I took her coffee order and gave him an encouraging smile, which wasn't reciprocated. I will mention that in his performance review.

Chapter 5

THAT AFTERNOON, I HAD the office to myself. No sooner had I started to enjoy that thought when I heard the lift doors open. There were three businesses on the third floor of our office building – an accountant, an architect, and our thriving publicity-private investigator firm. I counted to five and heard no knock, then eight seconds, and I heard a tap and a door opening... the accountant had a visitor. I relaxed again.

I was working on a presentation for a publicity client, and for the next thirty minutes, it was blissfully quiet until my phone rang. I leapt about a foot off the chair. I answered it on the second ring, and a female voice panted the words, 'I have a date. What do you want me to find out?'

'Who is this?' I asked, knowing full well that it was Melanie.

'It's me, dopey; who else would it be?' exasperation laced her voice.

'I'm a busy private investigator and publicist, Mel, it could be anyone of a hundred people!'

'How many calls have you had today?'

I thought about it.

'Ed's had three.'

'That doesn't count.'

'OK, fine, one ... from Dom. So you've got a date, I assume with the stallion?'

'Yes, so I win the challenge!' Melanie gloated.

'I knew you would. He was checking you out when he delivered your ricotta ravioli.'

'Was he?' She sounded delighted, as if she didn't know. 'So what do you want me to find out?'

I sat back and thought about it. 'I don't know.'

'Well, haven't you got a textbook – detecting 101 – see what it says!' Melanie contributed.

'That's a great idea! It's next to my *How to Run a Publicity Company* book; hang on, and I'll check it.'

'Very funny. OK, I'll just remember everything,' Melanie suggested.

'Mel, that would be great. Notice the little things. You know, who calls him, how he reacts to the calls, how he reacts to other people, if you notice anyone loitering or being aggressive around him, that sort of stuff. Oh, and find out what sort of things he collects.'

'You mean like stamps?'

'Yes. He said he collects things he likes. So find out what that means if you can?'

'Sounds weird. I now have visions of embalmed bodies in his apartment,' Melanie groaned.

'Don't worry. I think you're pretty safe with Ren, I've been to his apartment, and it's clear of bodies. Oh, I know something you can ask … see what Ren thinks of Vince's ex-girlfriend – it may be useful before I speak with her.'

'Who's Vince?'

'Vince is Ren's best friend who's temporarily living with him because his girlfriend dropped him. Where is Ren taking you?'

'Out for drinks first, and then he's taking me to dinner. I don't know where. Hopefully not to his restaurant again. He said to dress up.'

'Woo hoo,' I teased. 'I haven't dressed up for ages.'

'Well, get Dom onto it.'

'He'll say he did that on the first few dates, but now he's paid his dues!'

'Men,' we said in unison.

'Got to go, Mel. Can you warn Ren I need to speak with him again? I'll keep it short and sweet this time; I'll call him tomorrow. Have fun, be careful and call me in the morning.'

'I will. Ciao!'

I hung up and looked at my watch. It was 4pm and I vowed to throw myself into Ren's case tomorrow; I was taking too long. I had to speak to a bomb expert, find the detonator and speak with some of Ren's work and soccer friends.

I checked my diary. Ed and I had a meeting first thing in the morning with the manager of the Water Conservation Campaign. I grabbed the water file; we had achieved a fair bit of media for their campaign, they would be happy. The meeting was really just a wrap-up and a chance to see what other business we could get from them. That was at 9am. I drew a line from 10am to 5pm in my diary and wrote Renzo. Ed had enough to keep him busy with finishing the film and working on *Memoirs of Summer*. If nothing else came in for another week, I'd be happy to have time to dedicate to Renzo's file. It never worked like that; it was either a feast or a famine.

~ ele ~

Watching three crime shows in a row is not a good idea when you live alone, albeit with your dog. Every sound could be an axe murderer or some whacko coming to make you a statistic. I turned off the television and went to the kitchen to rinse my tea cup. Atlas followed me to the bathroom, where he watched me brush my teeth, and to bed, where he watched me get in before he decided he would get into his basket. We smiled at each other when we were comfortable.

Fifteen minutes later, I sat up on full alert. I had heard a sound ... worse still ... so had Atlas. He was emitting a low growl, and all the hair on his back was standing. I got out of bed; I decided I would rather be killed investigating than waiting to be found. We tiptoed to the edge of the staircase and looked down. Atlas's tail started wagging.

'Hey!' Dominic announced, taking his key out of the door lock.

'Hi. You scared me half to death. I didn't know you were coming over,' anger rode me as my heart hammered.

His face dropped at my tone. 'Oh, sorry. Do you want me to go?'

'No, no!' I assured him. Atlas ran down the stairs to meet him. I took a deep breath. 'You scared me, that's all.'

He patted Atlas, took the stairs two at a time, and held me. 'Sorry, Jesse. Wow, your heart's going a hundred miles an hour.'

'I was watching the crime trilogy,' I confessed.

'Ah-ha, that'll do it every time,' he continued to hold me, his chin resting on my head, his hand rubbing my back.

'I'm OK.'

'Shh.'

I waited until he decided I was fit enough to be released. He didn't take my pulse.

'Sorry, I'll call from now on,' Dom said.

'No, it's OK, really.' We moved from the hallway into the bedroom. 'Atty the warrior dog was on duty.' I patted Atlas. He seemed pleased with the title and moved past us, stopping to sniff Dom's pants, then returned to his basket.

'Can I stay?' he asked.

'Of course, you don't have to ask.'

'Good. I'm just going to have a shower. You keep reading,' he saw the open book on the bed.

'How was your mom?' I called as he entered the ensuite.

'Good. She asked after you and invited you to come next time. I told her you had a client meeting tonight that you couldn't get out of.' I heard the shower running.

'Yes, a meeting with the crime trilogy,' I mumbled. Going to his mother's was an ordeal. Occasionally, I did my partner duty and put myself through it. His mother spent most of the evening asking when we would get married and have children. She had five grandchildren but needed another one from Dom, her youngest son.

Minutes later, he walked from the shower, still damp and naked and crawled into bed beside me.

'That was quick.'

'I'd rather be here than in there,' he said.

'So what's up?' I closed my book and turned to look at him.

'Nothing. Why?'

'You're here.'

'I missed you.'

'And …'

Dom shrugged. I watched him for a few minutes while he looked down at the duvet, thinking. Then it began, as I knew it would.

'You know,' he started, 'I don't understand why you don't want to move in together. I don't understand why you don't want to get married.' I could see him getting angrier. It was the result of a trip to his mother's house. He continued. 'We've been together for eighteen months now. I love you, I know it's right. What's holding you back?'

I went to answer, but he cut me off. He was in full flight now.

'Call it off if you don't feel the same way. Tell me to get lost and let me have a chance of meeting someone else rather than stringing me along!'

'Is that what you want, Dom? To be cut loose and to meet someone else? Do you seriously think I'm stringing you along?' I was getting annoyed now, too. We had had this fight before; it was nothing new. And it was one of the reasons I avoided his mother; she incited it.

He folded his arms across his chest. 'No, you know I don't want to be cut loose. I want to marry you or at least take the first step and live together. But obviously, you don't feel the same! Why is that?'

I sighed, exhausted all of a sudden. My anger dissipated, and I felt like crying. I usually only cried when I was frustrated. I could feel the anger radiating from him.

'Dom, we've talked about this before.'

'But I don't get it.'

'Yes, you do.' He went to speak, and I shut him down. 'Listen, just listen to what you are saying.' I placed my hand on his arm, and he bristled. 'This is not you talking. You are a confident, gorgeous man with a woman who loves you madly. You know there is no one else in the world for me, yet you go to your mother's place for dinner, and you come back neurotic, questioning my love for you and our future together.'

I was just warming up. 'You know I've been married before, and it wasn't great! I think sometimes people stay in marriages for all the right and all the wrong reasons, so I'm not saying I don't want to commit again, just not now. I have said this before, and I'll say it again since you need me to: I want to be with you until I die. I'll wear your ring and say we're married if you like. I'll call you Hubby, Partner, or whatever! I just don't want to get legally married just yet. And as for living together, if you want to move in, move in!'

I must have shouted it because Atlas raised his head. Or perhaps he was getting territorial; I hadn't discussed it with him first. I gave Atlas a sympathetic look that said he would still be the alpha dog.

'You could move in with me?' he said, his anger waning.

'You live in a small apartment with no yard for Atlas. Besides, my home is dog-proof.'

'So the dog takes priority?'

'Atlas is my fur child. He has been with me for three years; you've been with me for eighteen months. Yes, Atlas is in the lead.' I was over the conversation now. 'I've said all I can say on this subject, Dom, you're just looking for a fight.' I sighed and went for a bathroom stop to give him time to work himself up again or down, depending on how many beers he had to get through the evening. I returned minutes later, and he seemed diffused. I climbed into bed beside him.

Dominic covered his face with his hands and groaned. He dropped them to his lap. Neither of us said anything for a while. He slid down lower on the pillow next to me.

'I'm a dickhead,' he said.

'Yeah, but you're my dickhead!' I grinned.

He looked sheepish. 'Jesse, I'm sorry. My mother and sister got into me tonight about how you couldn't love me if you weren't prepared to commit, that I was wasting my time and so on. By the time I left, I believed them. I questioned our relationship all the way here. I had to come over to make sure ... '

'I was alone?'

'Partly,' he said, looking away, 'and to hear you put all that straight.'

I ran my hand over his chest.

'Move in,' I suggested.

'No. You're just saying that now because I've been a total idiot.'

'No,' I assured him. 'Since you suggested it a few months ago ...'

'Six months ago,' he interjected.

'Yep, since then, I've thought a lot about it. I think it would be great.'

He looked at me for a long time and pulled me closer to him. He reached over and turned off the bed light. We kissed. Then he stopped.

'Jess ... '

'Yes?'

'I'm sorry, sorry this happened.'

'I know how you can make it up to me,' I said.

He laughed. 'If you still think moving in together is for you, suggest it to me again later in the week, not now to make me feel better. I'll believe you then. If you don't bring it up again, that's fine too.'

He lay on his back, looking up at the ceiling. I moved onto my side and looked down on him. He buried his face in my hair and sighed. The tension dissipated. I moved my hand down his

flat stomach and kept going down further. He moaned; I took
it as a sign that he felt more secure.

Chapter 6

ED AND I SET up the water conservation client with water, a coffee, and a croissant, presented our campaign overview, and waved him off at the door one hour later. Once the lift doors closed, Ed and I looked at each other and grinned.

'Love your work,' Ed said.

'Love your work too, babe,' I fired back. We had just scored another six-month contract launching the same project into another region – and it was time to invoice for the first job – my favourite part! Of course, the downside was that we would be busy again, but it was better than sitting around wondering if we should start marketing ourselves.

I left Ed to continue on the *Memories of Summer* campaign and sent Dom a text message. He had been full of bravado this morning. I knew he would be as he tried to re-establish himself as confident and in control after last night's performance. I tapped out a message. *Have you booked a trailer for the move this weekend? Love Jx.* He wanted confirmation, and I wanted him to have it, so I pressed the send button on my phone. I was nervous about him moving in – it's much harder to move out if it all goes pear-shaped – but I was also secretly excited. It would be great to come home to Dom at the end of the day.

I checked the answering machine messages. Melanie called, boasting she had information to share. I called Ren first. He was the perfect gentleman and said nothing about Mel or his short-term memory loss. We agreed to meet at the café near where his car was blown up in one hour. I rang Melanie.

'What took you so long to call me back?' she exploded.

'Work. You know how it is ... got to eat, pay the rent, and keep Atlas in the lifestyle he's accustomed to. How did it go?'

'Good, really good,' Mel said in a slow drawl.

'That's great! So, will you see him again?'

'What? No, I don't mean it went well with Ren. He's a bit slow, but OK if you don't have to talk to him too much. I meant my sleuthing went well. I think I may be good at this. When you're ready to take on a partner ... '

That was the second offer I'd had in so many days. I barely had enough clients to call myself a private investigator!

'I'll bear it in mind,' I promised her. 'So, spill it!'

'Well, for starters, he collects the weirdest things. He likes superior vehicles, so he has a collection of them, including several Mercedes, a Harley and a Ducati motorcycle. He also has an amazing collection of vinyl records and baseball memorabilia. Plus movie posters, many of them autographed.'

'Oh,' I said.

'What? Isn't that what you wanted to know?' Melanie sounded disappointed.

'Yes, but it's kind of useless information. I was hoping he collected something sinister or priceless that may encourage someone to blow him up, you know, like Picasso paintings or rare weapons.'

'Oh, sorry about that. Anyway, I didn't notice anyone following us or wanting to thump him. But we met so many people, everyone knew him, and they all seemed to like him. I think he's generous letting Vince stay with him, especially since he didn't have a kind word to say about Vince's girlfriend.'

'Really?'

'Well, almost. He said he thought she was too good for Vince but then called her a ball-breaking tart. Lovely! But he wants her to take Vince back, so he'll move out.'

'You did really well, Mel, thanks.'

'But nothing you can use?'

'It is all useable because it means I can eliminate those lines of inquiry.'

'Well, that's a good thing!' Melanie sounded brighter.

'It is. Thanks, Mel. I'm off to meet Ren now, so I'll catch you later for a drink?'

'Excellent. I'll email you.'

We hung up. I was getting scared to investigate further if it meant shutting down my leads; there were so few. I grabbed my bag and keys. I needed to find who rang Ren just before the car went up in smoke, confiscate his phone, and speak to a bomb expert!

❧

Ren was right on time; he dropped into the seat opposite me. He was wearing a black T-shirt again and jeans. The fit was perfect and showed his physique; he obviously worked out. I was dressed in a suit, having met with the water client that morning; we looked out of place together. After we ordered coffee, I gave him a brief update on whom I had spoken to and where I was going with his case. It was brief.

'How are you coping with Vince living with you?' I cut to the chase.

He shrugged. 'OK.'

'Do you think Vince will get back with his ex?'

'Hope not,' he said.

'Why?'

He thought about it. 'Yeah, well, it would be good because then he'd move out. But she's the boss, he is completely walked over. He doesn't see that, but if he stays with her, he will become a carpet!'

I could see Vince being under the thumb. I asked him about his phone. 'Just before your car exploded, you answered a phone call. Do you remember?'

'Yeah, that's right,' he recalled.

'Do you remember who it was calling you?'

'No, I couldn't hear anyone on the line, so I told them to hold on while I went outside, but then boom ... the car blew up!'

'Before you answered, did you look at the screen to see who was calling?'

He thought about it.

'I usually do that, but I can't remember.'

'OK.'

'Why?' Renzo asked.

'I'm trying to work out how the car was detonated. I gave him the options that Officer Abingdon had suggested. 'So I need to take your phone and have it checked.'

A look of dread appeared as he stared at his phone like it would explode any minute.

'Or you could keep the sim card, I guess if you can't part with your phone, but I'd rather you didn't open it at all.'

'It's all yours, I'm not touching it.' He edged it towards me. 'I've been speaking on it all week!'

'It may not be the phone; I'm just covering all bases.'

'How will you find out?'

'A bomb expert.' I picked up the phone.

Ren sighed. 'When will I get it back? I don't want it back unless it's safe to use.'

'Don't worry. I'll have it checked and get it back to you ASAP. Is this your only phone?'

'Yeah. But maybe I should get another.'

'You may not need to. Just give me a day. Divert the calls to your restaurant if you like.'

He did it while I waited. We finished our coffees, and I asked random questions about his soccer team and friends. He reported that nothing else unusual had happened since his car was bombed last week. I made some mental notes and kept it brief; I planned to let him go early for his good behaviour towards Melanie!

'I need you to think about who might have called you that morning at coffee,' I said as I drank my last mouthful. 'I know you said it was a bad line, and you couldn't hear properly, but did you hear anything?'

'Nothing,' Ren answered. 'I told them to hang on the line until I got out of the café.'

'So, if we went back through calls received, could you recognise any numbers that aren't normal?'

'Yeah,' he agreed. 'But the caller probably used a barred ID.'

'Probably,' I shrugged.

'Do you want to do it?' I offered him his phone.

'You can,' he passed it back to me without a show of chivalry or heroics.

I pressed the buttons on his phone with a bit of trepidation and went back through the calls received, looking for the date and time of the calls.

'You only received one call that Sunday between 10am and 11am.'

'Who was it from?' I heard him catch his breath.

I looked up at him. 'It says Vince.'

Chapter 7

The bomb squad was located in a sober, low-rise, brick building that stepped out of the seventies. There was no signage, not that I expected a neon sign, but a street number would have been handy. After a short-lived panic that I was going to be late because the building had disappeared, I found the public entrance and arrived with one minute to spare. The receptionist sat behind the security glass and looked relaxed and groomed; I looked stressed and windblown.

I asked for Meg Owens and was directed to the waiting room. I sat in a black plastic chair in a room best described as a holding room rather than a waiting room; it was sterile. Within a minute, Meg arrived. I guessed punctuality was important when it came to bombs. Meg was dressed in black pants and a red T-shirt that read, *I'm a bomb expert. If you see me running, try and keep up.'*

'Cute shirt,' I said.

'Thanks, we think it's pretty funny!'

I guessed she was in her late thirties but had seen some sun and looked leathery. She was easily a foot taller and wider than me and shook my hand assertively. I followed her down the hall and into a small, bland office. At least she had a window.

'Coffee, tea, water?' Meg offered.

'No, thank you. I imagine you're busy, so I'll keep this short and sweet.'

'It's been a big month,' she agreed.

'For bombing?' I asked, surprised.

'For lab work.'

'Oh.' I then told her about Ren's car, and she logged onto her computer and accessed the electronic police file.

She made a knowing sound, a cross between an 'Ah-hem' and a 'Hmm'.

'Mercedes! A write-off,' Meg announced.

'Can I pick your brain?' I asked.

'Sure.'

'The driver, Renzo, took a call on his phone moments before the explosion. Could it be connected?'

'Absolutely,' she said. 'The most inexperienced bomb maker can wire together a phone and detonator; it is pretty straightforward tradecraft. And, phones make reliable detonators because the terrorist can ensure that only a call from his phone number will cause the bomb to 'ring', so to speak.'

I nodded, fascinated. 'Can it go wrong?' I asked.

'Sometimes, they might accidentally ring the phone and prematurely detonate it. And yes, they have one major weakness, which is jamming. Jammers prevent the phones from ringing and, therefore, stop the detonation. It's been known to happen. Our troops use jammers in Iraq,' Meg continued. 'We can air-drop a phone jammer to knock out all mobile phone traffic in a combat zone.'

'Sorry, you'll have to be layman for me. How does that work?'

She smiled as though encouraged by a keen student. 'The gadget – this jammer – detects mobile phones near a convoy, then rings the number and, by doing so, detonates any potential bomb before our convoy gets too close.'

'That's brilliant!' I exclaimed.

'Exactly. There are so many benefits, for want of a better word, for using the mobile phone as a detonator.' Meg was getting into it now. 'For example, the battery has enough power to provide the energy needed in a detonation, it can be very precise in its synchronisation, and the Lithium-ion battery used in a phone can be turned into a bomb!'

I was starting to glaze over now.

'Israeli security forces are making their own phones with the handset rigged to emit a barely audible tone so that when the phone rings, the almost silent tone acts as a command code to detonate. There's also a mobile phone battery that conceals the bomb and it can be remotely controlled to explode. You would want to answer that with a long headset on!'

I think Meg made a joke, so I nodded and half smirked in agreement. I felt that covered a few bases. I took Ren's phone from my purse and gave it to her. She flipped it open.

'The bombs that exploded on the Madrid commuter trains were triggered by phones hidden in backpacks left aboard the trains,' she continued to share her knowledge.

'And what was the trigger in this case, do you think?' I nodded at Ren's phone.

'Is this the phone he was speaking on when the car exploded?' she asked.

'Yes.'

'Then it is not connected to the phone. This phone would have had to be next to the bomb – in the car in this case – and then a call would have triggered the bomb. Of course, it could have been the phone's alarm as well. This can be set to trigger the bomb.'

'Right,' I scrambled to make sense of it. 'So, the phone could not have been the detonator or it would have been in the car and burnt to a cinder?'

'Precisely.'

'Damn. That means I now have no detonator and no lead on how the bomb was set off,' I said aloud.

She looked at the electronic police file again.

'No, you have a detonator here,' she said.

I looked up and then looked at the screen. 'Where? What?'

'The police report found a burnt pager in the car. There's your detonator.'

'Really?'

'Yes. Pagers have a better range than phones because they only need to receive small amounts of data. They can also be concealed more easily because of their size.'

'And most beepers are anonymous to purchase,' I said, offering my small bit of knowledge.

'True. It's the same process you would use for a phone; the beepers give you a longer window – a few weeks compared to a week for a phone – and it can be set off from anywhere in the world.'

'The bomber would need access to the pager, wouldn't they?'

'Yes.'

'So would there be any evidence in the pager to suggest it had been used as a detonator?'

'Not necessarily, because it was just programmed to react to a ringtone.'

Major information dump! I had to go away and process this.

It had to be someone who had access to Ren's pager! And Vince was still the lead player.

'Water, water everywhere and not a drop to drink!' Ed exclaimed as I walked into the office.

'The Ancient Mariner!' I answered.

'No, well, yes, smarty pants, but I was thinking more of our water client. He just rang and wants to do a press conference in two days.'

I groaned. 'Good on him. OK, I'll organise the press conference and media release. I assume you're up to your neck in *Memories of Summer?*'

'Hmm, memories of something, but it's not summer!' he agreed.

We heard the lift doors open and looked up with expectation. There was no noise at the other two offices, so we expected someone was coming our way. Officer Jason Abingdon entered.

'Ah-ha, so this is where you hide out. Had a hell of a time finding you,' he grinned with a glance around.

'Your detecting skills paid off; here we are, Officer Abingdon,' I said as I stood to greet him.

'Jason, please,' he said.

I introduced Ed, and the men shook hands.

'Please, have a seat,' I directed him to our palatial leather couch near the window and sat on the other end. 'What's new?'

He pulled a piece of paper from his pocket and looked at it. 'I thought you might be interested to know that Ren's buddy, Vince Palino, has a rap sheet that is a mile long. It's just pissy teenage stuff, though: speeding, fighting, a bit of break-and-enter, but no major theft other than car parts. Except for one incident a few years ago ...'

Jason paused. I'm sure it was for drama.

'What happened?' I obliged.

'He blew up his father's car. Claimed it was an accident; he got materials mixed up that accidentally made a lethal cocktail while tuning the car.'

'Anyone buy that?' I asked.

'No. But he was let off with a fine. However ...'

'Damn, there's always a "however",' I frowned.

'Ren was with him at the time. They were playing around together on the car or playing with fire more like it.'

'So Ren's got a rap sheet too?'

'No. Vince's father didn't press charges, but Ren's name came up when I read the statement.

I thought aloud. 'You don't suppose Ren has blown up his own car for the insurance?'

'He wouldn't be the first to do it,' Jason agreed. 'Ren could have done it to collect the insurance, Vince could have done it for Ren, or Vince and Ren could have done it together. The possibilities are endless, or at least there are three.'

I laughed.

'Hmm, so Vince and Ren have been playing with fire ... or sugar as the case may be.' I looked at Jason. 'Thanks for that. You didn't have to come all this way to tell me that, but I appreciate it.'

'No problem, I needed to get away from the office and thought I may take you up on that coffee.'

I could feel Ed looking at me.

I nodded. 'Sure, I've got time for a quickie.' Wrong choice of words. I could feel Ed's eyes widening. 'Ed, I'll be back to start the press release ASAP,' I said, implying that time was of the essence.

'You've got thirty minutes before I lock you out in a bloodless coup,' he clued in.

'How'd you go with the bomb squad?' Jason asked as he followed me out of the office.

I smiled at Jason as we headed to the lifts. 'Got so much info, I'm a bomb guru!'

❧

'A half-strength skinny cappuccino and a long black,' the waitress put the coffees in front of us.

'Do the baristas here ever get aggro with you?' Jason asked after nodding his thanks to the waitress.

'What for?'

'For ordering half-strength? It's kind of like the woosy person's coffee!'

'Get out!' I said. 'I only order half-strength when I'm on my second or third coffee for the day. But now that you mention it, I did have one guy who kept making them a little stronger each time ... like he was weaning me onto stronger coffee. I soon fixed that, though. Dropped him and went somewhere else for coffee.'

'Ruthless!'

'That's me,' I agreed.

We both sipped our coffees.

'So,' Jason nodded to my hand, 'no ring, huh? Hard to meet men in the PI business?'

My instincts went on full alert. I wanted to keep Jason as an ally, but blowing him off now, when he's about to ask for a date, would make for a short-term business relationship!

'I've been there, done that,' I told him. 'I married a good friend who became more than a friendship, and then I realised maybe we were just friends. But he's still a friend.'

'Well, that's pretty good. Not many of us stay friends with the exes. Is Ed your new guy?'

'God no! Ed's got a boyfriend.' It was time to declare Dom's existence and see what happened. It might be a quick coffee. 'I'm seeing a personal trainer.'

Jason smiled.

'I know, sounds cliché, but he wasn't my trainer. I met him while studying some weekend subjects at the college.'

'So, do you train with him?'

'Occasionally. You know what it's like – if you spend the day doing something, like personal training, you don't want to do it after-hours.' This wasn't quite true. Dom was keen to train me after-hours, but I was keener to run on my own without him riding my ass. 'What about you? There is no ring on that finger, either. Got a partner in your life?' I asked.

Jason sat back. 'Not this week.'

'Last week?' I smiled.

'Hmm, let me think ... no. But I did want to talk to you about a family matter.'

My heart rate quickened. This seemed odd; surely he won't ask me out now that I've mentioned Dom.

'This is going to sound stupid ...' he began.

I shook my head. 'I doubt that. I work in publicity and investigation. I've heard everything stupid there is to hear.' I told him about *Memories of Summer*. I was stalling. He laughed at my description of our client. I vowed to make it up to Elizabeth for using her for comic relief.

'Sorry, I've digressed.'

His smile faded. 'Yeah. Well, I have a matter that I wanted to get investigated, a personal matter outside of the service.'

My heart leapt for joy! No date, new work! I tried to look solemn and encouraging.

'OK, what is it?'

He drew in a lungful of air. 'I've thought about hiring a private investigator but never felt comfortable telling all of this to a stranger. I wasn't quite sure I wanted to know the outcome and then I met you and thought, well you seemed pleasant and balanced, perhaps you would be discreet and would be the ideal person for the job ... assuming you want it and have time to take it on of course,' he added.

I nodded.

'Uh, where to start?' he said. 'I'll give you the abridged version and then if you want to take it on, maybe we can make another time to go into detail and work out a fee?'

'Sounds perfect,' I agreed. *Get on with it!*

'OK. My parents married when they were eighteen but couldn't have children. I don't know why; even IVF didn't work for them. But years later, after they had given up, Mom fell pregnant at 36 years of age.'

I nodded my understanding.

'Mom died when I was six. I was raised by my father, my aunt, and my mom's sister. She moved in after Mom's death to help Dad around the house and just stayed. Mom was sick for about six months before she died. I remember her being home in bed all day. I would come home from school, and she would be lying in bed, white as a sheet, with a stack of pill bottles next to the bed.' He stopped to sip coffee. I waited.

'She died one day when I was at school,' he stopped, swallowed and cleared his throat. 'I know this is probably nothing, but a few months ago, my father passed away. My aunt has gone into an aged-care home. She's just had her seventieth birthday and has the onset of early dementia.'

'I'm sorry,' I nodded, encouraging him to go on.

'Anyway, I've inherited the house, my old family home. So I've been dropping in after work some nights and weekends to sort through stuff. Dad's a hoarder ... I swear he's kept everything since birth.' He cleared his throat again. 'I came across these letters; they were love letters from my aunt to my Dad, and he has kept every letter. Of course, I knew they were romantically involved, but these letters were written when Mom was still alive. Since then, I've started having these memories of Mom saying things to me that, at the time, things I didn't understand. Now, I could be completely on the wrong tangent ...' he paused.

'You don't have to justify it to me,' I encouraged him. 'Just tell me what you are thinking, and we'll work towards finding the truth.'

He nodded. 'I remember one day when I got home from school, I was sitting on the bed with Mom, and she told me to call the police; she said they were killing her. I told Dad, and he dismissed it. He said Mom wasn't well and we had to make allowances for her. Finding those letters ... I know Dad's not around to defend himself, but ...'

He stopped talking and looked away.

'There's no one left to pay for the crime now,' he said eventually. 'If there was ever a crime, but I have to know for Mom's sake so that someone was on her side, I guess, to put her to rest.'

'I understand. I would do the same thing.'

'Would you?'

'I would have to know.'

'Thanks, that's how I feel. So will you take it on?'

'Yes, of course, if it eases your mind and helps you move forward,' I agreed.

He nodded, unable to speak for a few moments.

'But if you don't like what I find ...'

'I've thought about that. I'll deal with it,' he assured me.

I asked him what he could afford and suggested a fee schedule.

He pulled two separate wads of letters, tied with a red satin ribbon, from his jacket.

'Should I leave these with you? It's some of the letters I found ... or is that just a waste of time?'

'No. Leave them with me. I'll have a read of them before we next meet. I'll keep them safe.'

'Thanks.'

We agreed to meet at his father's house late the next day.

I dropped into the health club where Dominic worked to catch him before he left for the day. I hoped to talk him out of lycra and into jeans and to come for a drink. He normally took one-on-one clients in the morning for personal training, then attended either a school or club to give nutrition and exercise lectures during the day. He finished the afternoon at the health club, conducting fitness classes for the after-work crowd.

I waved to Jane, the receptionist and pointed upstairs. She was serving a customer but smiled and nodded. I headed up the stairs, where I could watch the class from the balcony. Dom wasn't hard to miss. He wandered around motivating students as they worked the gym equipment in the circuit class. The class was mainly female, and many played up to him.

Dom smiled or laughed at their comments, encouraging them along. Some girls were sweating and pushing themselves hard; they were there for the workout, not the flirting. It was odd watching Dom interact with them; he touched one of them on the arm, and my hackles went up. I was pleased to see him wander over to encourage a few guys and push them harder on their weights.

He glanced at his watch and gave them a five-minute countdown.

'OK, last five minutes, make it count,' he jumped on the climber next to one of the guys and did the last five minutes with him, increasing the pace and counting it down as they went. They struggled to maintain the pace with him.

'That's it,' he yelled. The class stopped with a groan, people stumbled off machines, and others bent over or wiped the sweat from their faces.

'Good work, everyone,' Dom clapped. 'See you next session.'

'If we can walk,' one of the guys shot back.

Dom laughed. 'You'll walk! Just think about what you are eating before you arrive,' I saw him glance at a couple of the girls. 'No afternoon chocolates. Go for a banana or a protein shake if you can't make it through between lunch and dinner!'

He saw them off, and I leaned over the balcony, waiting for him to spot me. He looked around, picked up some stray towels and glanced up. A grin spread over his face.

'Two clients, you are on fire!' Dominic pulled me closer on the couch at our local hotel. He was showered and looked irresistible in a fitted white t-shirt and jeans.

'Yep, I'll be putting on staff soon,' I smirked.

Dominic chuckled.

'So, packed yet?' I asked.

He groaned. 'About that move ...'

'Don't tell me you've changed your mind.'

Dominic shuffled in the chair. 'No, but ...'

'It's OK if you have,' I continued. 'But that's not to say I don't want you to move in.'

'I just want to be sure it's what you want as well and that you are not humouring me.'

I took a sip of wine and frowned at him. 'I'm hoping for some humour ... '

'You know what I mean,' he smiled.

'Look, it's not like we're getting married. If it doesn't work, you move out again,' I shrugged.

'Hmm.' He didn't sound impressed.

'Besides, I'm looking forward to it. A man around the house to kill the spiders, carry the heavy groceries in, take the rubbish out and for regular … '

His eyes widened. 'That I can guarantee!'

'… regular lawn mowing.'

'Oh. That too, I guess.'

⁓ℓℓ ⁓

I slid the ribbon off the aging letters that Jason had given me and shuffled through them. I opened the first one. It was from his Aunt to his father.

My dearest Charles,

I can think of nothing but you. I am sure I have not had a sensible thought in days. If only … I'm trying not to feel guilty for what I know is wrong. I can't bear the thought of causing my sister pain, but I can't stay away, and God knows I have tried. I know I will pay for it in the afterlife, but for now, I'm too weak to be without you. That is how deep my love and affection run. A meeting today?

Esme x

I was sorry for Esme. I couldn't imagine how I would feel being in love with Dominic and unable to have him. But I truly loved my sister, and nothing, and I mean nothing, would make me hurt her for my own selfish needs. I read the next letter. It was from Jason's father to his aunt. I knew straight away why Jason was suspicious.

My darling Esme

It is agony for me to be with Isabella and desperately want you in every atom of my being. I may have a solution that I will talk about with you. I think you should take up Isabella's suggestion to move in. Since she has been stricken with these terrible headaches that the doctor calls migraines, she is unable to get out of bed some days; I'm sure it would be a great comfort to her to have your support. I can't express how I would feel having you in the same house, being able to see, hear, and touch you. I have checked her medication, and being a pharmacist, I'm sure I can assist with more treatment to make it easier on her.

Yours, Charles.

My sympathy swung. Poor, poor Isabella – struggling with the belief that her husband and sister, the two people she probably trusted most in the world, were prepared to betray her. I couldn't even begin to think of the agony she underwent, knowing she might be leaving behind that little boy.

Chapter 8

I STOOD ON THE doorstep of Jason's father's house. I could feel the eyes of inquisitive neighbours on me, or perhaps I just imagined them peering from behind lace curtains. Jason had been called away on a job. I had the key, and I let myself in. A wave of stale air hit me as the house breathed in the fresh air from outside. It seemed familiar: the faded couches with crochet rugs over the arm pieces, the old floral wallpaper, small ornaments and a row of photographs along the top of bookcases. It was like my Grandma's house: neat but fussy. Like all grandmothers' houses, I guess.

The door slammed behind me, and I whirled around. Just the wind. I was in a Stephen King novel. The house was way too quiet, and knowing Jason's mother and father were now dead, Aunty Esme was in an aged care home, and a cup of tea was probably out of the question didn't help the mood. I moved to the photographs and looked at them. I recognised Jason in a number of the shots. At the back, there was a photo in a timber frame. I reached through the other frames and brought it forward. It must have been Jason's mother; a young boy sat on her lap, her arms wrapped around him, and they smiled at the camera.

Behind it again was another family photograph, this time with the three of them in it. I picked it up and studied it. Charles, Jason's father, looked conservative. He was wearing a brown suit and cream shirt with a red tie – very seventies, it wasn't a good look then and still isn't – at least he wasn't in a white suit doing a John Travolta impersonation. Jason's mother, Isabella, wore a long paisley skirt with swirls of pink and lilac colouring and a matching lilac t-shirt. Her hair was long and worn down, straight. She was attractive in an Ali MacGraw *Love Story* kind of way. No doubt that was the fashion of the time. Jason was in front of her in the photograph; her hands were on his shoulders. He had inherited some of her finer features: the delicate jawline, bright blue eyes, small nose and mouth. I put the photograph back.

I turned back to face the room; I didn't know what I was looking for, I just wanted to be here like a psychic going to the scene of a crime to see if they can feel something. I wandered into the kitchen and pulled out a few drawers. Everything was left in place as though they were expecting to come back. I was looking for the medicine drawer; every household has one. I have a medicine, hardware and bills drawer! I knew it was a long shot expecting to find anything that Jason's father could have used to poison his mother to still be in the house, but leave no stone unturned. Wasn't it Sherlock Holmes who said that?

I found the medication drawer and then hunted for a plastic bag. I found a drawer full of them. I placed all the medications in a bag. I didn't worry about fingerprints, they were only going to be Jason's father, Esme's or mine. I left the bag on the kitchen table and walked up the hall. There was a bedroom on the left done up in lilac colours, another on the right with the same colour theme, the third bedroom in a blue colour scheme and then the bathroom. I did the same again here, grabbing the few bottles of pills and lotions in the bottom drawer.

I returned to the main bedroom, a large lilac collared room with the old timber wardrobes and a dresser with a big gilt mirror. I wandered to the window to look out. It looked onto the backyard, where a huge oak tree took up most of the garden. A white bench seat was below it. I imagined Jason's mother lying in bed, looking out at the tree, maybe watching Jason playing in the backyard, knowing she was dying, believing her husband was killing her. I was overwhelmed with sadness for her. I turned back, and the bed was empty, of course; I shivered; her presence was nearby, watching me. I wanted to tell her I would find the truth for Jason. With more practice, I may not get so emotionally involved in the future.

'You are a star. We'll talk tomorrow, ciao for now,' Ed was on the phone as I entered the office. He rolled his eyes as the conversation continued, and he had another attempt at winding it up.

I grinned and indicated the kettle. He nodded.

'That sounds like a good idea,' Ed said. 'I'll see you tomorrow at the official opening. Be there nice and early ... yes ... yep ... righto ....'

I poured boiling water into two mugs, dangled the tea bags, and finished with milk. Ed was still trying to get off the phone. I dumped the bag of medications onto the desk and pulled out the first bottle. I sat down, logged onto the computer and researched the medication.

Ed hung up. 'Aggggggghhhh!' he moaned, 'Summer will never be the same for me ever again.'

'*Memories of Summer*?'

'Yes. We officially open the exhibition tomorrow, and we did two radio interviews and a local press interview this morning, and Ms Summer did well. But it has gone to her head. She's now a star. She thinks I'm her agent, not her publicist; she'll call me to pick up her dry cleaning next.'

'Hang in there, it's almost over. Then we can bill her, and you won't hear from her again until her next show – *Memories of Winter*? You might feature in it!'

'Spare me. We got a new client this morning,' Ed waved a file at me. 'A film company wanting publicity for a soon-to-be-released art house film.'

'Hmm, we haven't had one of those for a while; they must have a budget.'

'It's a tough film about a gay artist and his country's abhorrence of his lifestyle but not his work.'

'What a quandary!' I said.

'Indeed.'

'With your current workload, are you OK with doing it yourself?' I asked.

'Sure. I've got the water campaign well and truly underway, and *Memories of Summer* is just about done, so no problem. Are you snowed?'

'I've got two cases now, but I can help if you need me.'

'Two cases!' Ed exclaimed. 'Well, well, Ms Detective.'

I smiled and indulged his teasing. 'Yeah, well, Ms Detective wants lunch. Feel like some Italian?'

'Is this a working lunch?'

'Could be if Renzo's in the house.'

Chapter 9

Vince's ex-girlfriend, Yvonne, lived on the first floor of an old three-storey block of brown-brick units. Each floor featured a bay window and a central bright red door with a brass knob that looked particularly inviting. The top floor appeared to be an attic with smaller, hood-like windows. Across the road, a small gated park stood in the middle of the square. The street was smattered with parked cars. A small gold Honda CR-V was parked outside Yvonne's window, and I wondered if it was hers. I noted the registration number for good measure.

I ran up the stone stairs and looked down the list of names assigned to each doorbell. There were six in total, so there must have been two apartments per floor. I found Yvonne Benedetto's name and rang the doorbell. She had better be good-looking since Vince said we were alike, or he would pay. Yvonne was expecting me and buzzed me in through the front entrance. Inside, I found Yvonne's apartment to the left. The door to her apartment was royal blue with the same brass knob.

I was just about to knock when she opened the door.

'Yvonne? Hello, I'm Jesse.'

'Hello, come in,' she stood aside.

Yvonne was attractive, lucky for Vince, with a full figure, but not large. She was about my height, with shoulder-length dark hair and fitted clothes showing off ample cleavage, much bigger than mine. I could imagine Vince missing that!

Light spilled into the apartment through the bay window. Two large trees in sandstone-coloured pots sat on each side of the bay window, drawing your eye to the trees outside. Yvonne had good taste; the occasional plush cushion was covered in a gold and navy print, a bookcase full of hardbound books, and carved mahogany chairs were placed strategically around the room. I could live here. Two beautiful but worn hat boxes sat in one corner.

I settled on the couch while Yvonne made coffee. I sized her up while I patted her white, fluffy cat that was leaving fur on my tailored black pants. 'Sugar?' she called.

'Yes, just one, please. I'm trying to give it up.'

'I've got artificial sweeteners.'

'Perfect, thanks.'

'I'm always trying to give something up,' she walked towards me with the two cups of coffee. 'I was born dieting; I've got the

Italian genes and cream sauces to contend with,' she smiled at me.

I liked her.

'Fluffy, move along,' she instructed the cat.

Good name, it suited Fluffy, I thought. *If only we could all have names that described us.* I left that thought alone, returned my attention to Yvonne, and accepted the coffee from her.

'Thank you. As I mentioned on the phone, Ren hired me to investigate his car bombing.'

'Weird,' she shook her head.

'I know, I saw it happen,' I slipped into gossip.

'Any idea who did it at this stage?' Yvonne asked.

'No. I'm still talking to people, including the bomb squad and police.'

'So how come you are talking to me?'

'Well I met Vince, through Ren of course, and I guess I'm trying to get an idea of their relationship, from a different angle,' I told her.

'We've broken up,' she stated matter-of-factly. 'About three weeks ago.'

'He told me. He's not handling it well.'

Her face softened. 'I know. He came over last night, and he's called nearly every day. You don't think Vince did it, do you?

I can tell you he wouldn't hurt a fly,' she rolled her eyes, 'he wouldn't be organised enough to do it!'

'Why not?'

She sighed. 'He always has several projects on the go but never finishes anything. I mean, he has good ideas, just never sees them through.'

'Would he want to blow up Ren's car?' I asked.

She stopped sipping her coffee and looked at me, surprised. 'No way. They've been best friends since they were kids. I just meant that even if he did, and he wouldn't, he would never make it happen. Know what I mean?'

I nodded, confused.

'So, do you know Ren through Vince?'

'Sort of. We all went to the same high school, but I never knew Ren well until I started dating Vince.'

'What do you think of him? Ren that is. Do you know anyone who may want to do this to him?'

Yvonne sat back and thought about it.

'He's a bit of a man's man. You know, he hangs with the boys and is good to his buddies. He's always been good to them.'

'And the girls? Is he nice to you?' I saw her eyes narrow, and her lips get thinner.

'Hmm. Ren is also a ladies' man. He thinks women should cook, clean, look gorgeous and open their legs for him when it suits him.'

I decided to push my luck. 'Has he ever hit on you?'

Anger swept her face.

'I mean, you're a gorgeous-looking lady, and he would be exposed to you regularly,' which seemed to soften her.

'It's a bit of an issue.'

I waited; I had tapped into something here. My detective's skills were on full alert.

Yvonne continued,' He's come on to me several times over the last few years. Vince never knew. But ...'

I gave her my full attention, not interrupting in case she shut down.

'Recently, we had a fling,' she looked away and blushed. 'This time, Vince found out.'

'How?' I asked.

'He guessed it.'

'When?'

'Just before we broke up; it was why we broke up.'

'So he found out before Ren's car was blown up?' I confirmed.

'Yes, but I'm sure there's no connection. Honestly, Vince wouldn't do that,' she said again.

'Does Ren know that Vince knows?'

'I doubt it,' Yvonne looked alarmed. 'No, I'm sure he doesn't. If Vince had asked Ren, trust me, Ren would have denied it.'

'I'm sorry to ask you this, but, um, was it a one-off with Ren?'

Again, she stiffened.

'Strictly between you and me?' Yvonne asked.

'Won't go any further than this room,' I promised.

She hesitated.

'No, it wasn't a one-off. It started about a month ago. Vince was away for two weeks on business, and I went to Ren's Italian restaurant for a takeaway. Ren was working that night and invited me to stay and eat with him. He had to eat anyway, he said. Well, you know, he can be charming and after a few red wines and ... well, we went to his place.' She leaned forward, 'He was fantastic, and I mean fantastic! He made Vince look like a one-trick pony, if you know what I mean?'

'I know what you mean,' I nodded, willing her to go on.

'We ended up spending the weekend together, then a few more nights that week, and then the Friday night. Vince came home Saturday.' She sat back again and sighed. 'I could seriously be with him. But he doesn't want the same from me,' her face hardened. 'But when Vince came home, I couldn't bear to be with Vince. I know men can cheat with no remorse – it's physical, not emotional for them – but I couldn't be with Vince when my head was full of Ren. I was impatient with Vince, and I just wanted to be alone. I broke it off; I told him we had run our course. That's when he guessed what was going on.'

'But you don't think he's challenged Ren about it?'

'No. He's living there, isn't he?'

I left her question unanswered, assuming it was rhetorical.

'And you haven't heard from Ren since Vince moved into his home or since you broke up?' I continued.

'I've called Ren a few times since we split, but he hasn't returned my calls. He's an asshole.'

I nodded. 'And even though Vince thinks you have had an affair with Ren, he wants you back?'

'Yeah, well, we've been going out for a long time, and you know, I guess it's not the first time he's lost a girl to Ren. He's prepared to forgive me.'

'So Ren's stolen Vince's girlfriends before?' I clutched onto something she had said that smelled like a motive.

'Sure. But he hasn't stolen them; Ren doesn't want a relationship, he just beds them.'

There was enough motive for Vince to want to knock Ren off.

'You don't think Ren should come clean with Vince?' I asked Yvonne.

'No. It's bad enough that Ren did me over. There's no need to hurt Vince anymore than necessary. They seem to be able to get on together, living in ignorant bliss. If Ren doesn't admit it, Vince doesn't have to confront him.' She put her cup down on the placemat in the centre of the table. 'I know what you are thinking,' she said.

'What?' I asked, surprised.

'You're thinking, was it worth it?' Yvonne answered.

'No. I was thinking about how the sexes are different. You are right, what you said before … men seem to be able to do that and walk away; women usually make an emotional connection.'

She agreed.

I finished my coffee, and we sat in silence for a few seconds.

'Was it?' I asked.

'Was it what?' she asked.

'Worth it?

'Maybe,' she smiled. 'I'm pregnant.'

My lab friend picked up one bottle of pills after the other, studied the labels and returned them to the plastic bag. I watched him as he dismissed each bottle. Carl and I had known each other for nearly fifteen years since college. Carl was doing Honours in a Bachelor of Pharmaceutical Science degree, and I was doing a Marketing degree. Normally, we wouldn't have met; different buildings, different crowds, but we both played on the University volleyball team and what he lacked in volleyball skills, he made up for now in pharmacy skills.

He sat back, sighed and looked at me.

'Nuh.'

'Nuh, what?' I pushed him.

'There's nothing in that lot that would kill a person. Want a drink?'

I looked at my watch. It was 11.30am.

'It's nearly lunchtime,' he shrugged. 'Let's go for a beer, fish and chips. There's a good diner around the corner. Just like old times.'

'We never had beer, fish and chips,' I tried to recall ever doing that.

'Didn't we? I wonder why. Come on.' He rose and grabbed a leather jacket off the back of his chair. Standing at his full height of six foot four, Carl was a giant. He was not quick on his feet but great for those stray volleyballs that were too high for everyone else. He had filled out since our college days and wasn't such a bean pole anymore. In fact, he was looking pretty good in his jeans with a good choice of shirt.

'You've got a girl, haven't you?' I blurted.

'Yeah. Why?'

'Because you're looking good, I mean, you're dressed well,' I stumbled.

He grinned. 'So before that, I was ugly, huh?'

I thought of Melanie.

'No,' I assured him. 'I've got a friend ...' I began.

'Thank God,' he cut me off.

'Very cute. But seriously, I have a single friend, Melanie, who could be compatible with you, so if you find yourself single ...'

'Has she got a great personality?' he grimaced.

'No, but she's gorgeous.'

Carl laughed. 'Pray tell, how would you describe me to her?'

I sized him up again. 'Tall, fair and handsome. And if you give me any leads I can use for my case, I'll throw in some other adjectives, too!'

He grinned. 'Thanks, but I am seeing someone ... and it's getting serious.'

'Well! Good for you.'

We walked towards the front of the pharmacy.

'Just give me a second,' he excused himself to me and walked towards one of the girls on the counter to tell them where he was going. I looked around the shelves.

'Let's go,' he said from behind me.

'So, who is she?' I prodded.

'Who?'

'Short-term memory loss! The one you are getting serious about.'

He glanced back at the store and nodded. 'That's her working at the counter. Harlow.'

'Harlow?' I repeated.

'Yep, cute, isn't it? Her mom used to work at the Princess Theatre and saw all the matinees. So all her siblings are named after stars; not cliché names like Marilyn, but surnames. She has a sister, Monroe, and a brother, Gable. Sounds better when you meet them in isolation, though; it's weird when you're introduced to Harlow, Monroe and Gable in one whack.'

We turned the corner, and the diner came into sight. I looked at Carl again and wondered why, at college, I never realised what a makeover could do for him. Then, he was gangly with greasy hair; Harlow had done a fine job making him dateable.

The diner was filling up fast, so I dropped into a bench seat opposite him, which offered a view of a wall covered in sporting trophies and press clippings. The waiter came by, and we ordered the same, except for the beer.

'Back to me, me, me!' I teased.

Carl laughed.

'Tell me more about the drugs I found?'

'OK. They're a mixture of herbal tablets, aspirin-based products and general pain relievers.'

'But what if you took them in large quantities? Couldn't that kill you?'

He waited while the waitress put his beer and my white wine down before continuing.

'Cheers,' he said, and we clinked our glasses.

'Yes,' he swallowed. 'If you took the whole bottle of aspirin or painkillers, it probably would do you over … but this wasn't a quick death, was it?'

'No. It was gradual. Like a gradual poisoning. The husband was caring for the wife while allegedly killing her slowly.'

'Allegedly,' he smiled. 'You've got the detective lingo happening. Well, unless he managed to get her to swallow almost a bottle a night, the effects would be negligible.'

'So what am I looking for?' I asked.

'You're looking for something that can be added to a food or a drink that may be tasteless but slowly destroys the system. Something like that would most likely be available by prescription only. So rather than find the bottle, find the prescription, or her GP may be able to help,' Carl suggested.

'The GP's long dead, and the husband was a pharmacist.'

'Ah-ha,' Carl exclaimed. 'There's your problem. The butler did it!'

I laughed. 'As a detective, you make a great pharmacist.'

'OK,' he continued, 'who's your client? Any relation?'

'Yep, the deceased's son.'

'Good. See if her son can get her medical file if it still exists. They may release it to next of kin if he applies via the Freedom of Information Act.'

I pulled out my pocket notepad and jotted that down.

Carl continued. 'Did he work in a pharmacy or own the pharmacy?'

'I don't know, I should have asked that,' I realised.

'OK, if he owned the pharmacy and it's still in the family, see if you can check supply records. What did they get in and run out of quickly in the three months preceding her death? If the pharmacy is no longer in the family, it is worth trying his former employer if you can give them a date range. Try for her autopsy report ... if there was one...'

'Why would they do an autopsy?' I asked.

'They may not have. Suspicious deaths, suicides, etc, get autopsies. They may not have in this case because she had a prolonged illness ... but it is worth a try. See if she was ever admitted to the hospital and ask if the toxicology reports still exist ...'

I wrote down his suggestions in hurried shorthand.

'That do you for now?'

'Carl, you are wonderful. That's given me enough to do for a month. Thank you!'

'Good luck,' he said.

We spotted the fish and chips coming our way.

Chapter 10

THE REMOVAL TRUCK WAS pulling away from my driveway as I came down the street. It was official; Dom had moved in. I didn't realise how much he had moved in until I opened the front door and could barely find him for the boxes.

'Hi honey, I'm home,' I said.

'Me too!' he said with a look of sheer happiness.

'Welcome home,' I went up and kissed him. He grabbed me in a hug. Atlas joined in.

'This is kind of nice, isn't it?' Dom leaned on a box.

'It will be,' I looked around, eventually resting my gaze back on him as he stood in track pants, a t-shirt and his hands on his hips, sizing up where to put all his stuff.

'It will be great,' I assured him. We can come home to each other every night, share the cooking, hang around or go out; the possibilities are endless.'

Dom laughed. 'Let's get a takeout tonight, and I'll keep unpacking.'

'I had fish and chips for lunch. But I guess another load of carbohydrates won't kill me.' I momentarily forgot that Dom was a personal trainer.

'Yes, it will! We'll do steamed vegetables instead. Who did you have lunch with?'

'Carl.'

'Carl,' he repeated. 'Carl. Carl the mechanic?'

'No, that's Craig. Carl the pharmacist.'

'Pharmacist ... can't remember him.'

'I'm not surprised. Last time you met him, you both consumed enough pale ale for a small nation.'

'Oh, that Carl!' Dom pulled the tape off a box.

'Yes, that Carl,' I removed my jacket and shoes. 'He's given me some great insights into Jason's case. I've got to get back to Ren's case, though ... even though I would rather work Jason's at the moment, it has me hooked.'

'It's like kids and pets; you can't have favourites,' Dom said, pulling a large, ugly vase out of a box.

'Where did you get that from?' I stared at the vase.

'Engagement present.'

'Hmm, the engagement you piked on. How do I know if I accept your marriage proposal that you won't get cold feet and pike on me?'

'Because you know I'm mad about you.'

'And you weren't mad about her?' I pushed. I didn't want to know, but I couldn't help myself. OK, I did want to know.

'No, I wasn't. We dated in high school, and we just kept going. Everyone expected us to get married. It just seemed the logical thing to do until I realised neither of us was really in love with each other. We were just a habit.'

'Did she have a dog?' I asked. I saw Atlas's ears go up.

'No,' he directed the answer to Atlas while still holding the ugly vase.

'Why didn't you give her the vase or return it to the sender?'

'I tried. But she didn't want it, and since it came from my side of the family and they were sorry for me, they didn't want their gift back,' he looked at it more closely and sighed.

'Don't worry,' I shrugged, 'there's a cupboard in the kitchen big enough to lose it in.'

'We can be like the Queen,' Dom suggested.

'Ed?' I joked. 'He's always claiming that title for himself ... the big drama queen!'

Dom laughed. 'No, the Queen of England. I hear she keeps a register of gifts, and should a dignitary visit, the gift they gave is whipped out and displayed. Then you think it meant something to her. We'll whip this out if Aunty Eunice drops in.'

'I've never heard you mention Aunty Eunice?'

'She's grandma's sister.'

'That would make her in her eighties at least?'

'Exactly. So she won't be over that often,' Dom assured me. 'She may be dead now that I think about it, or was that Aunty Thelma?'

'Clearly you're a close family,' I headed upstairs to change.

Atlas walked past us, his head down, not making eye contact.

'He's got one of your socks in his mouth.'

'Which box was he into?' Dom asked.

I pointed to the small one in the corner.

'Um, that's not a sock ...'

I couldn't sleep. Keeping as quiet as possible, I rose, closed the bedroom door behind me and snuck along the hallway to the study. Atlas lifted his head from his basket in the lounge room, saw me stalking down the hallway and went back to sleep. I flicked on the desk lamp.

My mind was working overtime with the information Carl gave me. Could Jason's father have killed his mother using poison that he was able to get through the pharmacy without anyone noticing? I knew the Centre for Drug Evaluation and

Research monitored drug development and effects, but did they require every pharmaceutical purchase to be logged?

I did the calculations. Jason's mother died in 1978. Would there still be records going back that far? I wasn't optimistic.

I searched on the internet for poisons. I didn't realise how easy it was to kill yourself; just follow the step-by-step guides available online. Several poisons could easily have done the trick – but they would have shown up eventually in an autopsy – if an autopsy had been done. Surely, the family doctor would have run some tests, but how often did Jason's mother see a doctor? I made a list of questions to ask Jason about his father.

I sat back, feeling a bit lost. I decided to read through some more of the letters Jason gave me. I grabbed my work bag and removed the folder. Another pile of letters was tied up with a ribbon that I hadn't opened yet. Not that I was expecting any great insights, just more of the same display of affection. The first one I opened was faded and began to crumble around the edges. I carefully laid it on the table and scanned the letter. It was from Jason's father. He was away on business and writing from a hotel room, knowing the two women were home together. Nothing was revealed in the letter except for the continued adulterous sentiments.

I read four more letters. As the letters continued to profess their desire to be together, there was no doubt they deeply loved each other, but they revealed nothing more. I was starting to feel tired again. There were at least another ten letters to read.

I told myself, I'll knock these off and then go back to bed. Letter number five.

The hairs stood up on my arms as I read the first few sentences. I stopped, inhaled and started from the beginning again.

Not long now, my darling, until we are together. I know, I know ... I can hear you say be patient, but I have been, we have been, and my impatience is making me careless. I'm going to step her treatment up a bit ... increase the palliative care, and help her manage the pain better, faster.

I scanned the rest of the letter, which included the same professions of love that appeared in other letters.

Step up her treatment. Help her manage the pain better. I had to speak with Jason and find out what medical reports I could access ASAP. But first, I had to get working on Ren's case before he gave me the sack, or all my leads ran cold, or both.

Chapter 11

I SAT OPPOSITE RENZO, who wore his traditional black outfit from head to toe. He was handsome and charming; I could see why Yvonne would fall for him, especially since Vince was neither handsome nor charming. One of Ren's staff delivered us a cappuccino, and he looked up and smiled at the attractive waitress.

Yep, always on the lookout.

He watched her walk away, and I watched him. He turned back to find me staring at him. At least he looked appropriately embarrassed. I handed him back his phone.

'It's safe to use,' I assured him, seeing his reluctance to accept it. 'You have a pager?'

He looked surprised. 'Yeah, I had a pager. How did you know that?'

'Because it was found in your burnt-out car, and the police bomb squad are pretty confident that it was your detonator.'

'Holy shit,' he swore. 'I hardly ever used it. My father insisted on me carrying it because he complained that I was always on my phone and that he couldn't reach me. This way, he pages me, and I call him back.'

'Someone had to have access to it to make it the detonator,' I told him and watched that fact sink in.

'So, they couldn't just page me with a special code or whatever ...'

'No, they had to tamper with the pager first. Who had access to it?'

Ren looked up at the ceiling as he thought.

'Well, no one. I never take it out of the car. I know I should,' he glanced at his father behind the bar, 'but I'm not big on being traceable, know what I mean?'

'Sure do,' I agreed. 'So in that case, would the only people who would have access to the pager be anyone who had access to your car?'

'Yeah, but no one did,' Ren stated.

'So no one cleans it for you?'

'Oh yeah, I have a detailer who does it once a month, Peter from Glean-N-Clean, but he's been doing it forever and is a good guy. Why would he want to blow me up?'

'Nobody borrowed your car in the last few weeks?' I pushed on.

Again, Ren took his time thinking.

'Only Vince, that's it.'

'Vince? What for?'

'To impress some chick. He was going on a date. I felt sorry for him, and he'd just been dumped, so I loaned him the car.'

'How long did he have it for?' I asked.

'He took it after work, about six and was home by two the next morning.'

Plenty of time, I thought. *Vince was looking shifty again.*

'Would Vince have any reason to want to blow you up?' I asked matter-of-factly wondering if he would reveal his affair with Yvonne.

Ren lied like a professional, repeating what he had already told me. 'Nuh. He's my best friend, we've known each other since we were born, and he's currently living with me. Why would he want to knock me off? What's in it for him?'

'Maybe he's pissed that you slept with his girlfriend,' I hit Ren with it. He choked on his cup of coffee and reached for a glass of water.

'What do you mean?'

'You know what I'm talking about. I spoke to Yvonne,' I said.

'Why?' he snapped.

'Because you're paying me to find who may want to kill you and, so far, the runners-up are your best friend and his ex-girlfriend, who you had over two weeks before dropping her cold on Vince's return.'

'You're fired, forget it.'

'Really?' I grabbed my bag and slid out of the booth. 'Well, good luck when the next bomb drops.' *Arrogant twat!* I quickened my step, keen to get away.

'No, wait, wait,' I heard his voice behind me.

I didn't even turn around.

'Wait,' he called. 'I'm sorry.'

That must have hurt his pride to say sorry aloud. I stopped and turned around. 'Forget it, Ren. I'm not desperate for your work, you know.'

I've got at least one other client!

I pulled open the door. I also had too much pride.

'Jesse, wait, I'm sorry ... wait up,' he caught up and put his hand on the door to close it. 'You're right. I hired you, and you are doing a good job. I want you to stay on it.'

'OK,' I said. 'But from now on, you need to tell me the truth, Ren. Who is out to get you?'

━━ℓℓℓ━━

After leaving Ren, I counted three possible suspects: Vince, who Ren didn't think was a potential, but he was my lead suspect. After all, Ren took from Vince the one thing he loved, and according to Yvonne, it was not the first time. Adding insult to injury, he's living in Ren's luxury apartment, watching Ren get plenty of girl action and seeing Ren driving around in a luxury car while Vince is desperate and dateless. Jealousy is a well-respected cause for murder.

A long shot was Yvonne. She was jilted, but in my mind, she seemed pretty happy with the outcome. I expect she wanted a child, maybe Ren's child and at least Ren's alimony.

Finally, an unknown third party. Ren had been remiss in mentioning that he had also had an affair with a woman who turned out to be married to a well-connected family who didn't like Ren's type. He was threatened in the car park at his restaurant several weeks before to stay away from her or else. Ren assured me he hadn't returned to her, or, as he put it, "she wasn't that great a toss to risk that!" So again, that wasn't top of my list, which meant despite Ren and Yvonne's protestations, Vince was still up there. It was time to pay him another visit.

I parked next to Ed's car and turned off the ignition. I sat silently for a moment, thinking about my two clients, Ren and Jason. Ren was harmless; his life would probably be full of good-looking women, fast cars and easy money – the product of a happy home, a wanted child and a comfortable upbringing. Jason, on the other hand, had an edge of insecurity about him, the side effect of losing his mother at an early age. His life would always be one of work, commitment and loyalty while he searched for the things missing from his childhood home.

Give me a Jason type any day. Ren was way too flashy for me; it took all my willpower to continue with his case when, frankly, I didn't care who tried to blow Ren up, even if that sounded uncharitable.

I stepped from the car, locked it, and took the stairs to the office – the three flights were good exercise if it wasn't a hot day. Ed was sitting at his desk, a set of earphones on, typing away at his computer. He pulled out the earphones when he saw me.

'Hey, how's it going?'

'Good,' I slumped into my office chair. 'Could use a drink.'

'Coffee?'

'Can't we have a wine?'

Ed looked at his watch. 'Four o'clock. That's cocktail hour. Why not?'

I rose and went to grab two glasses. Ed selected a red wine from the cupboard and opened it. We had done this before.

'Any exciting long PR lunches that I've missed?' I asked Ed.

'I don't know,' he smirked. 'I'm a busy publicist. I've got this boss who never lets me do what I want and then forces me to drink with her in the afternoons.'

'Horrendous!' I agreed.

'Have you found who tried to blow up Renzo?'

'Nuh, but if I give you fifty bucks, will you do it?'

I clinked glasses with Ed and sniffed the red wine.

'Mm, nice,' I sipped. I loved a good Merlot, even if it wasn't trendy at the moment.

'Is Ren being obnoxious?' Ed asked.

'Just his usual self. I don't think Ren's used to working with women as equals. Most of the women he knows are waitresses, cooks in the kitchen or managing the home. He's finally met one who doesn't want to cook for him or bed him.'

'And can talk in full sentences and say big words,' Ed agreed.

We heard the lift doors open, and Dom stepped into the office shortly after.

'Oops, we're in trouble now,' Ed said, taking his wine glass back to his desk.

'Ah-ha!' Dom exclaimed, 'so this is what you two get up to early afternoon.' He grabbed a glass and helped himself.

'What resistance,' I teased him.

'Saves you twisting my arm,' he agreed. 'Solved Ren's case yet?'

I gave him a look that said exasperation.

'I'll take that as no.'

'We just had that discussion and you missed it.' I filled him in, including the fact that Yvonne was now pregnant.

'My most likely suspect is Vince, the best friend. I've got to go and speak with him again.'

Dom sat back on the leather office couch and extended one arm along its back. He rested his wine glass on his knee.

'I think I should come with you,' he said.

'Why?' I looked up, surprised.

'Does he suspect that you suspect him?'

'No. I don't think so.' I swivelled on my chai,r thinking about it. 'I don't think I've ever given him the impression that he's a suspect. But I don't think Vince ever intended to kill Ren. I think he was angry that Ren had taken his girlfriend and wanted to take something from him.'

'So he took Ren's love, so to speak ... the Mercedes,' Ed finished.

'Exactly,' I agreed.

'Have you got any evidence to incriminate him?' Dom asked. He turned to Ed. 'All these crime shows give you a great vocabulary ... I could be a detective, too.'

'I've got motive,' I shrugged. 'Two suspects with motiv,e actually.'

'So, does Vince know about the child – Ren and Yvonne's love child?' Dom asked.

'I don't know. I'll have to check with Yvonne. I don't want to ask him and find he doesn't know; he'll know then. You know what I mean?'

Both men nodded.

'I guess that's two motives for Vince – Ren cheating with his girlfriend and now the child,' Dom said, 'and one motive for Yvonne – desertion.'

'Plus,' I continued, 'Ren has a constant bevy of women, money and fast cars. Vince is scraping by, yet it's rubbed in his nose day in and day out. Might be different if Ren was really in love with Yvonne, but he's just done her and moved on.'

'I'd blow up his car too,' Ed said.

'Make a note of that,' I turned to Dom, 'Don't you hit on Simon, or Ed will come after your car.'

Ed agreed. 'I'll come after something, but maybe not the car!'

'I've got circumstantial evidence,' I continued, 'not enough to hang him, so to speak. Vince has a previous charge of making bombs; he blew up his father's car. Vince had access to Ren's car to tamper with the pager, which was the detonator.'

'So how do we do it?' Dom asked.

I smiled at him. 'I like the 'we', thanks.'

'I say we catch him in the act,' Ed said as he rose and topped up our wine glasses. 'He's tried once and failed. Why wouldn't he keep trying?'

'I think Vince will only keep trying if he is trying to kill Ren, and I don't think he is. He's succeeded at blowing up the car; in his mind, that may be a settled debt.'

'I think you should drop this case,' Dom said. 'He may try and get you off the scene as well.'

'No way. I can't drop every case where there's an element of danger. I may never get a job!'

'You know,' Ed thought aloud, 'Yvonne could have a motive. If she got rid of Ren and she was carrying his child, the child could inherit.'

'Maybe,' I agreed. 'But she also wins just by keeping him alive to keep working and paying alimony.'

The phone started to ring. Ed reached for it. 'This will be one of my film reviewers; I've got a film screening tomorrow,' he said before answering.

While Ed took the call, I turned to Dom.

'Maybe Ed's right. I need to catch him in the act or somehow get the confession from him.' I sighed. 'I'll sleep on it. Speaking of which, I'm exhausted. Want to go home to bed?'

'Now? It's only 4.30.'

'Too early? OK, forget it.'

'Grab your bag,' he said, heading towards the door.

Chapter 12

THE NEXT DAY, I entered the police station for a 9 o'clock meeting with Jason, Officer Abingdon, in his environment. I went to the front counter and was ignored for at least five minutes. Who would have thought 9am would be peak hour at the police station? People were coming and going, being bailed from the night before. Several were looking worse for wear, still harbouring hangovers; a couple of ladies looked sheepish to be seen in their spangly slips and high heels from last night's outing, and a couple of girls who appeared to be regulars to the jail were saying their farewells.

A tired-looking middle-aged police officer finally came to me.

'Who are you here to bail out love?' he asked. I looked down; I was dressed like a solicitor.

'Um, Officer Abingdon,' I answered.

The police officer laughed. 'Yeah, we've been saying he should be locked away for years.' He turned and yelled. 'Abingdon, visitor! Take a seat, young lady.'

'Thank you,' I turned to find all the seats except one take,n and it was next to a man I could smell from ten feet away. I decided to stand.

'Jesse, this way,' I heard a voice call. I turned to find Officer Abingdon directing me down the hallway. We entered a small room, and he closed the door.

'Is this where you interrogate people?' I asked.

'Yep. You can see all the marks around the walls,' he joked.

The room was brand new in keeping with the surroundings. Even though Officer Abingdon was my client, it was still scary sitting in a room in a police station with a police officer in uniform.

'Thanks for coming in,' he continued. 'I've got some stuff for you.' He pushed a box towards me. 'It may not be relevant ...'

'That's OK, I can weed out what is,' I assured him. 'What have you got?'

'Some of my father's medical notes. I tried to get Mom's medical records, but her GP is dead. In the surgery where he used to work, he only kept patient records for seven years. That was the legal requirement at the time, and as the receptionist said, there were no electronic files then, so they didn't have room to keep files forever. I went back to the pharmacy that my father used to own. Same story; they don't have stock records going back that far or a computerised record of my mother's scripts or my father's either for that matter.' He looked deflated.

'Autopsy?' there was no delicate way to ask.

'Not that I could find.'

'It was worth a try; thanks for that,' I said. 'So what is here in the box then?'

'The pharmacy had a box of stuff in their storage cupboard with my father's name on it. They said it hadn't been thrown out because there was some research stuff in there, including a published paper, so I guess someone thought it was worth hanging onto.'

'I'm surprised they didn't call you to see if you wanted it,' I added. 'Who has storage space these days?'

'I think it got lost there, and they just found it when I started making inquiries. It was in a room that used to be my father's lab,' Jason said with a smile. 'I remember as a kid going to the pharmacy and we'd go downstairs to the white brick room he'd call the lab. Dad was always experimenting with something. He used to say whoever came up with the cure for the common cold would go down in history forever.'

'Is that what he was trying to do?'

Jason shrugged. 'Don't know, actually. I was a kid; I just liked to look at the rats and snakes ...'

'Rats and snakes!'

'Yeah,' Jason said matter-of-factly. You can't do experiments without testing them. It's still illegal on people, you know,' he winked at me.

'I guess so. I'm just surprised ... grossed ou,t actually. Why the snakes?'

'Anti-coagulant.'

'Sorry, anti-what?'

'Snake venom is used as an anti-coagulant in blood. Not that my father discovered that, but I guess he was trying to find something like that. He always believed plants and animals produced all we need to survive as a species.'

'Logical, I guess,' I agreed. 'My mother always said the same about food. Whatever primitive man ate is what we are meant to eat today, not all this manufactured food.'

Jason nodded. 'Our parents would have gotten on well.'

I tapped the lid of the box. 'It's a good start. Leave it with me, and I'll get to work. I was thinking, if it didn't upset you too much, could we visit Esme at the aged care home and chat with her? I'm not expecting her to reveal anything, but it could be worthwhile.'

'Yeah, sure, I have no problem with that. I usually see her a couple of times a month anyway.'

'That's nice,' I said.

'How about next week?'

'Anytime is good for me.'

We rose.

'I'll carry this to your car,' he grabbed the box. I allowed him to be chivalrous.

—ⅇℓⅇ—

My phone beeped, and I read the message from Dom.

'Two hours free between classes. Coffee?'

I replied, and we agreed to meet at our usual place. As I drove out of the police station car park, I thought about Jason's case, which wasn't going that well. I didn't know how to prove his mother had or had not been poisoned. If it had happened in the last five years, our chances might have been better; at least we would have known what drugs she took or what Jason's father administered from the pharmacy on her behalf. I could have spoken with her doctor to get more of an idea about the symptoms she had if he was still alive. I could have tried to talk Esme into relieving her conscience if she still had a fully intact mind. I hated the thought of not being able to get a result.

I got a parking space close to the coffee shop. Dom was sitting at a table by the time I got inside.

'Hey,' he rose from his chair as I approached. It was a big week for chivalry. I slipped into the chair next to him.

'This is a nice surprise,' I held his hand.

'I've been thinking,' he started. 'About Vince.'

'Vince? Oh, Vince, sorry, I was immersed in Jason's case. One-track mind.' I leaned back as the waitress slid two coffees in front of us. 'Want to share a slice of carrot cake?' I looked at the well-iced, moist cake calling my name. 'It's kind of healthy; it has a carrot in it.'

'I'm ahead of you,' Dom said just as the waitress returned with a large slice and two forks.

'Excellent.' I would only have three bites, but they would be three large bites. Dom could afford to have carrot cake on his hips more than I could.

'Vince ... ' he continued.

'Mm, I'm listening,' I assured him as I studied my fork and the first mouthful.

'He's still in love with Yvonne, isn't he?'

I nodded. 'He said he hoped they would get back together, so I'm guessing he still loves her and doesn't know about the kid.'

'But what happens when he does find out about her being pregnant? If he was prepared to blow up the car when she cheated, what would he do if he found the child was Ren's? I think this is way too dangerous for you.'

'Dom, relax, I'm not going to get blown up,' I pushed the carrot cake towards him!

'I can't relax. Why don't you stick to publicity? It's much safer.'

'That's not true. I was nearly bored to death at a choral concert once.'

Dom laughed. 'At least do me a favour ...'

'What?' I studied him.

'Fill Officer Abingdon in. Just let him know what you have found. Ask him to watch your back. It is part of his job or should be.'

'OK,' I agreed.

'Really?' Dom was surprised I agreed so readily.

'Yes, really. I think that's a good idea.'

Dom looked pleased. 'Thanks, babe, I feel much better.' He leaned over and kissed me, then proceeded to polish off the cake. 'You are still convinced that Vince is the one who did it?'

'Yes. He had access, he had the skills, he had motive, and he was the last person to call Ren. Unless ...'

'What?' Dom put down his fork.

I sat back in my chair.

'What if Vince and Ren are in this together? What if they faked it for insurance or ... or it's a cheap publicity stunt for the restaurant ...'

Dom leaned in closer. 'OK, how would that work, and why would Ren hire you?'

I thought for a while. 'You're right, that's too much of a long shot, and I'm getting carried away now.' I threw my hands up. 'If it is not Vince, then I've wasted a fair bit of time and don't know where to start from there.'

We both sat in silence.

'I'm over it now,' I said to Dom, 'I've got to do some publicity work this afternoon anyway to give Ed a hand. It will make for a nice change.'

I grabbed a takeaway slice of mud cake to take back to the office for Ed. It was his favourite, and the sugar rush would put him in a good mood for the rest of the day.

Driving back to the office, I quickly called Melanie; I was playing a hunch. As an accountant for a financial services firm, she had access to financial records that the average private investigator couldn't access. She rang me back a few minutes later and informed me that Ren had no outstanding loans on his car or any of his collection of vehicles. That ended that line of thought; no sharks were chasing him, back to the drawing board.

I took the lift up to the office since I was carrying cake – it made sense, and on walking in, Ed looked pleased to see me.

He was doing his bit to brighten the office in an orange shirt and brown pants.

'Thank God you're here,' Ed started.

'Sorry, are you swamped?'

'No. I just couldn't bear working on the water client alone. Now we can share the joy.'

'And as luck would have it,' I smiled at him, 'I'm just in the mood for water.' I put the mud cake in front of him.

'Bless you,' he said, staring at it fondly.

I grabbed the file and plopped myself down at our boardroom table. Ed followed suit.

'Let's do it,' I opened the file.

The sun was just starting to dip below the skyline when I left the office. I decided to drive past Ren's place on the way home. I had to speak with Vince again soon but didn't know where to take that conversation. I hoped looking at where he was living would inspire me. I might even drop in if the lights are on. I slowed down as I approached Ren's apartment building and looked up. The lights on the floor were off. I was relieved. Just then, the front door of the first-floor foyer opened, and Vince came out and made his way down the stairs. I kept driving, but looking back in the rearview mirror, I saw him walking down the street. I came to the end of the block and swung the car back around to follow him. The '*Conduct surveillance*' subject in my investigation course now had a chance to be implemented. What a shame I couldn't instigate the '*Coordinate surveillance vehicles*' subject ... I could have had Dom, Melanie and Ed on duty!

By the time I came back around, Vince had entered a liquor store. I parked and waited. He came out with a few beers and a bottle of wine. He didn't head back to Ren's place; he kept walking. I watched him from my parked car for as long as possible and then pulled out. He walked one more block before heading into a small Thai restaurant. I pulled over and watched, trying to be discreet. At least he didn't know what car I drove. The restaurant's interior lights were on, and I saw him being led to a table. He handed the waiter the wine and one of the beers and kept the other beer. He sat by himself, picked up the menu and looked over it.

I wondered if he was having dinner by himself or waiting for someone. Given he had bought wine, I guessed he was expecting female company.

I looked up and down the street and couldn't believe my eyes; Yvonne was walking towards the restaurant. She pulled open the door and went in. Vince smiled and waved; she went straight to his table, kissed him on the lips, not cheek, and sat down.

Were they back on together? It pretty much looked that way. Or were they never apart?

~ele~

After stalking Vince, I had a craving for Thai and called my favourite Thai restaurant to order a takeaway. Dom picked it up on his way home. I poured the wine and set up our cutlery in the lounge room, anticipating his arrival; routine queen!

He had barely walked into the house when Atlas and I accosted him with hugs, licks and kisses. Atlas did the licking. I was dying to talk through what I had seen, and I filled Dom in while we served. When I finished, he was grinning at me.

'Well, what do you think?' I asked.

'I think you're the cutest detective I know,' he kissed me.

'Really? Thanks. How many detectives do you know?' We entered the lounge room and sat on the couch before the television to eat our takeaway. Atlas rejected his dinner and watched us, hopeful of a leftover even though he didn't like rice and thought the curry chicken was too spicy.

I continued. 'I think it's a setup.'

'Go on,' Dom took a mouthful of chicken curry and nodded his appreciation.

'I think Yvonne was angry because Ren dumped her, not that she told Vince that. But she has sided with Vince to get Ren. I think Yvonne is pregnant with Vince's kid but I believe that she is faking that it is Ren's child to bribe Ren to pay her, you know, to shut her up. Then she and Vince will take the money, move and be well set up, never to see Ren again.'

Dom nodded while he thought about it.

'Could work,' he agreed. 'But what if Ren doesn't believe it and asks for a paternity test? If Vince is the father, then Ren's screwed.'

'True, if he asks for a paternity test. I think he'll pay to get rid of her because he is the last person in the world who wants to settle down, and he definitely doesn't want to be with her, from all impressions. I'm going to fill Ren in on my theory.'

Dom's eyebrows shot up, and he stopped eating. 'Jess, do you think that's wise?'

'If I don't, he might be bribed and not tell me. I want to prep him, and then he'll tell me whatever happens. I think if Vince or Yvonne bribes him, we've got them for blowing up the car.'

'You're making me nervous,' Dom wiped his mouth with the paper napkin.

'Really? I'm pretty excited.' I refilled our glasses. 'And I've got a huge box of stuff to read for Jason's case!'

'Jason?'

'Officer Abingdon,' I corrected myself.

'Hmm,' Dom said suspiciously. 'You won't have time to read it tonight; I've got plans for us.

'Do tell?' I teased him.

'Do show, more like it,' he grabbed the television remote. 'The game's on!'

Chapter 13

'Shit! I don't believe this,' Ren ran his hands through his hair. We sat in a booth at his restaurant. It was 11am, an hour before the lunch rush hour, and I gave Ren my theory. I broke his pending fatherhood to him gently, but he wasn't taking it well.'

'No way,' Ren shook his head, 'you're off the mark. It can't be mine.'

'Well, if you wore a condom, then there's a good chance it's not yours,' I suggested.

He rubbed his hands over his face.

'It is only a theory,' I said, guessing there was no condom used. 'I could be completely wrong. Vince may not know, and ...' my voice trailed off, knowing that even if Vince didn't know, Ren would still likely get a call from Yvonne about the pregnancy.

'Christ,' Ren banged his hand on the table.

'Has anyone threatened you since the car bombing?'

'No.' He sat looking stunned. 'Vince wouldn't blackmail me.'

'So, there's no way Vince would do that to you, his best friend?'

'No way. He wouldn't.'

'Because you're loyal and trustworthy and great friends don't screw each other's girlfriends?' I reminded him.

Ren looked around. 'He doesn't know. Do you think Yvonne will tell Vince it is his?'

'You better hope she doesn't. Anyway, I'm only telling you this because I suspect you are about to get a call soon from Yvonne, and if you do, I want you to tell me because it could incriminate them both.'

He nodded.

'You have to promise me you won't say anything to Yvonne first; you won't tell her that I told you?' I instructed.

Ren didn't say anything.

'Ren!' I got his attention. 'You'll blow this case if you say something to her. I'm the only one she's told. We have to see what happens; if they are in it together, let her come to you.'

Ren nodded. 'OK.' He brightened, 'She may change her mind and decide to convince Vince that he's the dad.'

'She might,' I agreed unconvincingly. 'Just remember, it's only a theory. Even if Yvonne does contact you, then there is nothing really to say that she and Vince are in this together.'

'Except that you saw them dining together,' he reminded me, 'and he told me he was going to see his mom last night, not Yvonne.'

'Except for that,' I agreed.

❦

Dom had two evening classes – high-impact aerobics and boxercise – so it was the ideal time to relax on the couch with a nice glass of red wine and dark chocolate. At my feet, I had Jason's box from his father's pharmacy. Atlas lay in front of me on the rug, hogging most of the heater. He stretched and then resumed his former curled-up position.

The television played in the background so I could divide my concentration between the news and the box of papers.

I leaned down, pried off the box lid and found it three-quarters full and dusty. I grabbed a pile of papers from the top and sat up.

'OK, what great insights could I hope for here?' I said aloud.

Atlas raised his head off the floor, looked at me for a few seconds, sighed and put his head back on the rug.

'You relax, I'll let you know,' I told him.

The first few pages were letters from Jason's father to editors enquiring if they were interested in publishing test results from an experiment. I kept flicking through. More correspondence from journals, a certificate acknowledging completion of a course, a statement agreeing to publish his results and a prescription ... my heart rate momentarily increased ... nope, just a prescription for aspirin and an order form for a range of vitamins. I finished the first pile and put it beside me.

'Nothing there, Atty,' I told Atlas. I knew he wanted updates.

I reached down and grabbed another bundle. The paper was brittle on some of the documents, and they flaked on the rug.

The first few pages were much the same. The next was a large document bound in a plastic folder. The title read *Mind-body Interventions and the Effect of the Human Immune System* by Charles Abingdon, BSc (Pharmacy). I yawned. *This will be a good read, no doubt*, I thought with a sense of dread. I looked for the executive summary, but there wasn't one, so I began with Charles's introduction. The thesis was an experiment on how the immune system worked and how it could be conditioned through the mind.

OK, hold on!

I realised the importance of what I had in my hands. I sat up and started reading from the beginning again, paying more attention this time. Charles had experimented to prove that the immune system could be psychologically conditioned to perform a certain way. I had to get my head around this; he was trying to prove that the mind could be used to weaken or strengthen the immune system. I got a rush of goosebumps.

I flicked through to the actual experiment. Charles fed four rats a formula of saccharin.

Saccharin, isn't that just sugar? I rose and went to the study to grab the dictionary. I returned and found Atlas had moved from the rug into his basket, allowing me to share the heater.

'Thanks, Atty. I'm looking up saccharin.' I flicked through and found the definition. There was saccharide, which was any sugar or other carbohydrate and saccharin described as excessively sweet; sugary of the nature of or containing sugar and there was a definition for saccharin – a sweet white crystalline slightly soluble powder.

I went back to Charles' thesis. When he gave the rats the saccharin, he also gave them an immunosuppressive drug that caused them to feel sick in the stomach. *Poor rats.* I hated animal experiments, but that was a can of worms I didn't have time to open. I went to the results. The rats soon learned not to touch the saccharin because they started associating it with stomach discomfort. Charles kept experimenting and found that the more of the stomach-upsetting drug he gave them, the more they avoided the saccharin as they connected them. The next page was the bibliography. I shuffled back through the pages; that wasn't right. What happened after that? Did the rats' immune systems stop working? Did they think that the saccharin would kill them, so eventually it did? I looked along the edge of the document. The pages had been torn out.

That's weird. Why would someone tear out the results? Unless they were incriminating. A cold shiver ran up my spine. Maybe after Charles had finished experimenting with rats, he had moved to humans. Just one human.

~ elle ~

Dom came home several hours later and woke Atlas and me; we had fallen asleep in the lounge room. After two hours of working out, Dom was full of energy; I probably had enough energy to climb upstairs and bed. I went upstairs to shower before bed, while he ate the dinner I left for him in the oven. He was watching a comedy, and now and then, his laughter drifted up the stairs. He had a rich laugh, deep and infectious.

I remember dropping into bed, but I don't remember Dom coming in beside me. I woke up with a start at 2.13am according to the digital red lights of the bedside clock. I could feel my heart thundering; I reached for Dom – he was there. I rolled over and snuggled in behind him. I had been dreaming about Isabella. She refused to take the medicine, and Charles got angry. I could feel her desperation and panic. She knew he was killing her and that she was alone. She was trying to get a message to Jason, but he was too young to understand. I wondered if that's how she really felt and if she resigned herself to death. I felt miserable at the thought.

I ran my hand down Dom's arm. I didn't want to wake him, but I wanted him to be awake. I could feel the tautness in his arm, the muscle definition and the fine layer of hair on his arms. He moaned beside me. I couldn't imagine wanting him to die. I couldn't imagine standing by and letting someone else slowly poison him. How could Esme do that to her sister? If it did happen, I reminded myself. There must have been years and years of resentment between her and Isabella. Or maybe her love for Charles was all-consuming. You hear of that kind of love, where women help men murder or rape other women because of love; it defies explanation.

I felt a wave of love for Dom. If he had asked me then and there to marry him, I would have said yes with conviction. It was a good thing he was still asleep. I wondered what Isabella could have done to save her own life. She could have spoken with her doctor ... unless he was a good friend of Charles. Who would have believed her over a respected pharmacist? They would have thought it was the illness talking or she was going mad. They probably would have pitied Charles and admired how he and Esme looked after Isabella.

What would I do? I would leave him, get out and go somewhere. Where? Would I be well enough to leave? What about Jason? Would you try to take him with you? I would be scared to leave him behind, but if you thought you were dying … and it was the seventies, there were probably a lot fewer help services around then. Dom stirred.

'What's wrong?' he mumbled.

'Nothing,' I whispered.

'Are you cold?' he turned and pulled me into him.

'No. Bad dream.'

'Not the chocolate chasing you again?'

'No. That was just when I was dieting.'

'One of the cases?'

'Yes. It's OK. Go back to sleep.'

He snuggled in closer and kissed me. He tasted warm.

'You're safe, go back to sleep.'

I sighed, feeling the tension leaving my body.

Chapter 14

I wanted to see Carl, the pharmacist, again. I gave him a call, and he was happy to meet. I offered to pay for lunch in a more upmarket restaurant this time in return for picking his brains, and he vowed not to eat breakfast and save his appetite. I invited him to bring along his girlfriend in case she thought I was hitting on him; it was important to keep the girls on side. He didn't, however, and showed up right on time, wearing a tie.

'You look swish,' I complimented him.

He grinned. 'I thought I better make an effort in case they refused to serve me.'

The waiter sat us near a window overlooking the park and lake. The tablecloths were crisp and white, and the wine glasses were enormous. We ordered a glass of wine each and perused the menu.

'Are you having an entrée?' he asked.

'Well, normally I would scrap the entrée and share a dessert with Dom, but given most men hate sharing dessert unless forced to by their girlfriends, I'll go the entrée and no dessert.'

'I'll take that as a yes then,' he summarised what I said.

'I'm going to have the grilled calamari salad and, for main, the grilled chicken breast,' I told him.

'Goody two-shoes,' he eyed the menu.

The waiter arrived, and I gave my order.

Carl inhaled. 'OK, I'll go the trio of dips with Turkish bread for the entrée, and for the main, I'll have the steak, please.'

'How would you like it cooked, sir?'

'Medium, thanks,' Carl answered.

'Sauce, sir?' the young male waiter continued.

'Uh, mushroom.'

'Vegetables or salad?'

'Vegetables, thanks,' Carl snapped the menu shut.

The waiter took the menus and departed.

Carl wiped his brow. 'The Spanish food inquisition!'

We clinked glasses and after a sip of the chilled wine, we got down to business. I told Carl what I had found. He listened with great interest; I was talking about something that had him hooked.

'So, what do you think? Did the saccharin eventually make the rats as sick as the immuno suppressant or whatever the drugs were and could it have killed them, you know, tricked their mind into thinking they were sick and then they died?' I stopped. 'That sounds a bit out there now that I've said it aloud.'

'Not at all,' Carl put his wine glass down. 'That's fascinating. What year did you say his thesis was?'

'Uh, it was in the early seventies. I can't remember the exact year. Why?'

'What was Jason's father's name?'

'Charles,' I told him, 'Charles Abingdon. Why?'

'Well, you will be interested to know that a well-known and similar experiment was also conducted in the early seventies. It sounds like Charles has run the same experiment to validate it.'

'Seriously?' I asked excitedly.

'Seriously. It was done in New York by two doctors. I can't think of their names. Hang on.'

Carl reached for his phone and opened the net search engine. He searched for two words – rat and saccharin.

'Write this down so you can do more research later,' he instructed. I grabbed my pen and paper.

Carl continued, 'Ronald Beckey, B-e-c-k-e-y,' he spelled it, 'and Philip Turner.'

I repeated it after him.

Carl read from the website information. 'Beckey and Turner discovered that the immune system could be psychologically conditioned to perform a certain way.' He looked up at me to ensure I was listening and then returned his concentration to his phone and continued reading. 'Beckey fed rats saccharin while simultaneously giving them an immunosuppressive drug that caused an upset stomach. Soon, the rats learned to avoid the saccharin because it made them ill. The more of the stomach-upsetting drug they received, the greater their avoidance of the saccharin.'

'Clever rats,' I added.

'Indeed,' Carl read on. 'The study was then repeated using only the saccharin and no drug. Beckey said he was surprised to find many of the rats died.'

'Just from eating the saccharin?'

'Yep,' Carl said. 'Beckey said he realised that even when the rats did not receive the drug, their bodies associated the saccharin with the suppression of immune function; so their immune systems became weaker. In other words, the more saccharin the rats received, the more likely they were to die.' Carl looked up, 'The moral of the story is the mind and the immune system are linked.'

'And Charles was doing the same thing, only to Isabella!' I exclaimed.

'Allegedly. I suggest that Charles was testing their experiment on a human ... but I wouldn't suggest that to your client since it is his father.'

I looked at Carl with dread.

'So let me make sure I've got this right. Even without the drug, the rats associated the saccharin with making them sick, and consequently, their minds suppressed their immune function, and therefore their immune system actually became weaker.'

He nodded, plunging his Turkish bread into one of the dips. 'The conclusion, therefore, is that the mind and the immune system are linked.'

'And Charles proved this on his wife ... death by sugar.'

'Maybe,' Carl said, 'and her doctor would be struggling to find what was causing her body to shut down when there were no drugs in her system.'

'That might just be the cruellest thing I've ever heard,' the weight of it pressed on my shoulders.

'I've heard much worse than that,' he doubled-dipped his bread. 'One more thing,' he added, 'given Charles owned the pharmacy, he could have coated both the saccharin capsules and the immune suppression drug with the same pharmaceutical glaze or coating so that they looked the same and administered these to his wife, she takes them, feels ill, but he assures her they are working and insists she must keep taking them.'

I had to get my head around this. 'OK, let me put it in layman or laywoman terms. It is possible that Charles gave a drug and saccharin to Isabella. Maybe they both had a coating so they looked the same and looked like pills. He told her it would help her ailment. She took them and felt sick. She began to believe he was trying to kill her and that the drugs were making her worse. Still, he forced her to have them, so towards the end, when he removed the drug and just gave her the saccharin capsules, she continued to believe it was killing her. Her immune system shut down, and she died. There would have been no traces of any drug in her system to incriminate him if they had done an autopsy.'

'Bravo, you'll make a doctor yet,' Carl raised his glass in a toast.

'I feel sick,' I said.

'Calamari no good?' he asked.

I gave him a look that I hoped said volumes.

'I know it's hard not to get emotionally involved, but think of the good you are doing,' Carl said. 'You may even get justice – albeit it posthumously – for Jason's mother.'

I raised my glass. 'To Isabella.'

'To Isabella,' Carl agreed.

Chapter 15

THE NEXT MORNING – a windy, wet day that made me grateful to have a car parking spot – I wrestled Jason's box of papers from the car and took the lift to the office; it was locked, and Ed wasn't in yet. I liked it when he beat me in and turned on the lights, kettle and heater. It was the same feeling as coming home to a warm house. I unlocked the door, flicked the light switch and placed the box on my desk. The phone rang while I was taking off my coat. It was a potential new publicity client – a charity group wanting publicity for their fund-raising fun run. I made a time to see them and hung up.

I put the kettle on and checked for messages. There were two for Ed from clients, plus a call from the municipal choir wanting us to publicise their next tour. They were a difficult client to promote because of their repertoires. If only they would tour with a selection of popular classics or Andrew Lloyd Weber covers – but no, they picked abstract classical numbers that interested purists only – and with the amount of choice today, people's entertainment dollar was spread thin enough without that challenge. Nevertheless, it was nice to have a steady stream of clients. I jotted down their details to call them back.

'Morning!' I heard Ed announce behind me. 'Cold enough to freeze your socks off today. Is that coffee you're making?'

'Morning, yes it is chilly and yes, coffee is on its way,' I greeted him.

I watched him unwrap layers of scarves, jackets, hats and gloves.

'Are you in there?'

'I walked here,' he explained, his face red from the cold.

'Why?'

'Simon has this thing about getting more exercise and fresh air, bracing the elements he calls it.'

'Life expectancy?'

'God knows,' Ed answered. 'Hopefully he'll be finished this fad in a week or less.'

'Must be love,' I said.

Ed saw my handwritten messages.

'Mona from the choir!' he groaned.

'Yes. There's one to look forward to.'

'What is it this time? Schubert Mass No 6 in E flat!' he rolled his eyes.

'Actually, that I could market.'

Ed studied me. 'You look tired. Too many late nights playing with Dominic since he moved in?' he winked at me.

'No. Yes. Some of that,' I confessed. 'The cases are keeping me awake. My mind's working overtime, and then I dream about them.' I poured the boiling water into two cups, added milk to the instant coffee and sugar to Ed's and placed one in front of him.

'Thank you!' he wrapped his hands around the cup. 'I'll need ten minutes to thaw out.' He nodded at the box on the floor next to my desk. 'Publicity or crime-fighting?'

'Officer Abingdon's papers. I'm almost finished. I thought I would bump them off this morning, so to speak. Then I'll call Mona back and that other one, too, the fun run lot. How are you going?'

'Excellent,' he said, logging into his computer. '*Memories of Summer* has paid her bill, the water campaign is well underway in two other councils, and the film is released this Thursday, so we're just waiting for the reviews. I'll take the fun run if you like.'

'Sold!' I slapped the desk. 'Thanks for that, much appreciated.' I tore off the phone number and walked it to his desk.

Ed was inhaling the steam from the top of his coffee.

'Back to crime-fighting,' I sighed.

Picking up Jason's box, I placed it on my desk, sat down and took the lid off the box. I pulled out the remaining papers. There were more articles Charles had written for publications and more handwritten notes about his experiments. The final document at the bottom of the box gave me goosebumps. It was the published copy of Beckey and Turner's experiment and the results. The same Beckey and Turner that Carl had told me about.

I sat back and thought about what this meant. Charles Abingdon hadn't been experimenting or writing a thesis about the immune system. He tested Beckey and Turner's findings and documented them. But he must have known his thesis could never be published because he tested on a human, and the results could implicate him for Isabella's death. He was keeping the data for his own curiosity.

So, were his recorded results from using the rats or from using Isabella as a guinea pig? I may never know. Even if I reported this to Jason, what evidence is there that he actually experimented on his wife? Sure, there are papers and reports, but that could have been reading material. Would it be enough for Jason to surmise that it happened?

Then I remembered Esme, Isabella's sister and Charles's second wife. She was our last living witness or the last living collaborator.

I took the plunge and called back Mona from the Municipal Choir.

'Hi Mona, Jesse Clarke returning your call ... yes, we would love to,' I assured her, grimacing at Ed across the desk. 'Bruckner's Mass in E minor, excellent.' I made a date and time to see Mona in person and wrote it in my diary. Thanking her, I hung up and groaned.

'Yeah, good luck with that one,' Ed grinned.

'Mm, I have two words for you: fun run!' I teased.

'Yeah, yeah, trust me, it is easier to get people into lycra than it is to get them to a choral concert.'

'Don't I know it?' My phone rang, and I looked at the number. Ren. I'm betting he's had a demand call from Yvonne.

Ren wanted to see me right away. It was a matter of life and death, he said, his not mine. We agreed to meet at the coffee shop where I spent my Sunday mornings and his car was blown up. He was a bit of a celebrity there now. I got there in twenty minutes, and he was waiting, wearing black.

'I've ordered,' he said, pulling out my chair for me. *Nice touch.* 'They knew what you normally have.'

Hmm, routine queen strikes again!

'Thank you. What's up?' I leaned in towards him.

He looked around, so I did the same. I'm not sure who or what we were looking for.

'I think you are right,' he said. It sounded great and I wished he would say it again.

He continued. 'I got a call from Yvonne yesterday afternoon …'

'What time?' I interrupted.

'Um, about four. She said she had to see me and asked if she could come to the restaurant that night. I agreed, and she came at nine. I couldn't see her before that, we're too busy. I wanted to call you afterwards but thought it might be too late.'

'Thanks,' I said as our coffees arrived. I stirred my cappuccino, hoping it was half-strength on skim milk.

'She told me she was pregnant, and according to her calculations, it had to be mine,' he rubbed his hands over his face and then took a gulp of coffee.

'What did you do?' I asked, knowing this part was going to be crucial.

'You would have been proud of me; it was an award-winning performance. Thank God you prepared me.'

I was about to say I didn't want him to lie or act any way but naturally, but I thought, what's the point?

'I told her that was fantastic, the best news I had ever heard.'

I almost spat my coffee on him.

'We didn't discuss doing that!' I exclaimed.

'No, but I thought about it for a long time after our conversation, and I thought I could either pretend to be shocked and run a mile – which is what I would have done if you hadn't warned me – or I could play into her hand and be thrilled and see what happened.'

'Not bad,' I said impressed. I had to hand it to him; it was a pretty good strategy. 'And?'

Ren smiled. 'You should have seen her face. She was blown away. I'm sure she expected me to disown her. It took the wind from her sails.'

'I'm sure it did. It's taken the wind from my sails. So what now? What did she do next? If she's in cohorts with Vince, now she has two partners!'

Ren continued. 'She stared at me for a long time. Then she started to say she was so pleased I was pleased, and maybe we could do this together.'

'What did you say?'

' I just shut up and nodded,' Ren said. 'I wanted to see what was coming.'

'I'm impressed, Ren,' I congratulated him.

'I thought – *screw you bitch, I'll win this*,' he boasted.

He just fell off the pedestal.

'She didn't say anything for a while,' Ren continued, 'I think I blew her away. So I asked for a paternity test.'

'Did you?' I nearly fell off my chair. 'How ... what ... what did she say?' I was glued to his daytime soapie life being played out live.

'Well,' he continued, 'she sort of changed tack a bit and started saying that it may not be mine and that it could be Vince's because she had only broken up with him two weeks before, and she would have to think what she would do.'

'Seriously?' I aske,d surprised.

'Yep.'

'Hmm, it mustn't be yours and she knows it, otherwise she would wipe Vince and grab the chance to do this with you.' I dreaded boosting his ego, but it had to be said.

He shrugged. 'Hey, she's only human.'

'So how did you part?'

'She's going to let me know about the paternity test. I sent her flowers today,' he gloated.

'What about Vince?' I reminded him.

'Well, if your theory is right, Vince knows the kid could be mine and wants to be in on the bribe. He'd expect me to deny it and want to keep it quiet. He would have his hand out, thinking I would pay to get rid of her. Now they're probably sweating trying to come up with another plan.'

I nodded. 'So I guess we need to wait for the next move from Yvonne. But we need to be careful about this. If we are right and Vince discovered you were having an affair with her, so they decided to blow up your car ...'

'Blow me up,' he interrupted with emphasis.

'Hmm, I'm not sure that he wanted to kill you. I think you took his best possession; he took yours. Anyway, we may not be able to prove that, though, with the evidence at hand. Let's face it, he's had plenty of chances to bump you off if he wanted to – he lives with you!'

'OK, maybe,' Ren was prepared to give up the drama element.

'There are at least two scenarios here. Vince has gotten over your cheating by punishing you. But when he realises Yvonne is pregnant with your child, well, he may get violent again.'

'And the second scenario?' Ren asked.

'It's the original theory that he's forgiven Yvonne, and they are in this together and figure there's a way to fleece you. Given I saw them dining together and I saw the kiss on the lips, my money's still on this theory.'

'So how do we find out?'

'I think it's time I chatted with Vince again,' I said.

I told Officer Abingdon—Jason—my theory on Vince and Ren. He was on a day off but still agreed to meet with me. We met in a coffee shop in his neighbourhood. He looked quite handsome in civvies: jeans, a dark navy corduroy jacket and a white T-shirt underneath. It suited his colouring. I was glad I wasn't in love with him; I would be scared whenever he left for work that he might not come home to me. We sat inside. The coffee shop had a fireplace and a good-sized fire going. It was particularly cosy looking out the glass window,s watching everyone hurrying by.

'Is there any way we can prove it?' I asked Jason for his thoughts.

'We could get a warrant for Vince's place, see if there's any evidence there, you know, material that could be used in constructing a bomb or a detonator,' Jason suggested.

'He's moved out and is living with Ren. Besides, he's been charged with owning this material before, so he may still have it but may not have used it.'

Jason nodded. 'Then, short of a confession or a witness, it's pretty hard to prove that one.'

'What if Ren had been killed? How would we prove it then?'

Jason thought about it. 'I guess since Vince had motive, he would face more interrogation, and we would be watching his body language, following through his alibis, and maybe keeping him under surveillance. We may be able to trace the substance back to a distributor, to his premises. You've done some of that where possible.'

'I have. My mini surveillance stint caught him with Yvonne, and his alibi on the day of the bombing checked out, but as we know, he didn't have to be there to set the bomb off.'

Jason shrugged. 'Given it is only vehicular damage and no injuries, we wouldn't waste the resources on doing anything more than what you have done.'

'So it has come down to me getting a confession,' I summarised.

'Yep. Then Ren would have to decide if he still wanted to press charges. It is his best friend, after all.'

'And an eye for an eye, more or less,' I agreed. 'Can we talk about your case, your dad?'

'Sure. What's the latest?'

'I don't think you are going to like my conclusions,' I ran through what I had found in the box, my chat with Carl and the information about the experiment.

He didn't say anything for a while after I finished and didn't make eye contact. I watched him, his mind ticking over, his jaw clenched as he fiddled with a teaspoon. I wondered if I should have delivered the news more sensitively or if I should leave now for him to process it.

He looked up at me and cleared his throat. 'Can we talk later?'

'Of course,' I assured him.

He pushed his chair back and rose. 'Thanks, Jesse.'

I watched him leave. All my clients, all two of them, were unhappy.

I picked up the sugar sachet. Sugar had played a part in both of them being unhappy: the bomb and the poison. I would never look at it again in the same light.

Jason called the next day; he wanted to meet with me again. We met closer to my place at the coffee strip a few blocks from the office. I loved this area. I sorted the street by category: the best coffee, breakfast, lunch, and superior carrot cake. This time, we picked the café with the best coffee and sat in a window booth.

I wrapped my hands around my coffee.

'Are you cold? Do you want to move out of the doorway?' Jason offered.

'No, I'm just taking advantage of the cup's warmth,' I told him. I was anxious about seeing him. I'm unsure if that was fear of his reaction, fear of hurting him, or lack of practice at delivering bad news that worried me. The worst news I could deliver in the publicity business was that we didn't get enough exposure or that they were about to cop a bad news story. Small dramas at the time, but they don't compare with confirming your suspicions that your father may have killed your mother.

'I'm sorry about yesterday,' Jason said.

'Why?'

He shrugged.

'There's nothing to be sorry about,' I assured him. 'I could have delivered the news better ... but remember, it's not proven, Jason; these are just circumstantial things I have found. Nothing is damning there.'

He nodded. 'It's pretty damning to me. You know, sometimes you remember things when you see them in a different light. I remember seeing my father and Esme in intimate situations while my mother was alive. I guess as a kid, you don't think much of it. Dad used to say he was comforting Esme because she was upset that Mom was sick but in retrospect ...'

I nodded and waited. I thought I would let him get everything off his chest before speaking. Perhaps I should have done counselling as a career.

'It all makes sense,' he continued. 'There's Dad and Esme having it off in one corner, Mom telling me she's being poisoned, Dad's experiments and having that immune system research in his hands at the time, and he treating her as well.' He looked out the window.

It was time to say something. 'It would be nice to know though, wouldn't it? I mean conclusively. Sorry to be direct, but what's the cause of death on the death certificate?'

'Organ failure,' Jason answered. He must have read that line a few times over the years.

'And there was definitely no autopsy done?' I asked.

'No. It wasn't required because she had been sick for some time and under a doctor's and Dad's supervision; there were no suspicious circumstances.'

'That's unfortunate,' I chose my words.

'Yes,' he finished his coffee. 'Want another?'

I looked at my cup. 'I could go for tea this time ... an English breakfast, please. It's my turn to buy, but it would just end up on your final bill anyway,' I tried to lighten the mood.

He laughed. 'I'll order,' he rose and walked to the counter.

I looked at my notes. OK, so there was no autopsy, no record of medication given or taken, and no record of quantities ordered by the pharmacy. No signed confession from Jason's father; just kidding on that one! Esme was our last hope.

Jason came and sat back down. 'On its way.'

'Thank you. We need to see Esme.'

'I know, I was thinking the same thing. But you know she has onset dementia,' he said.

'I remember you telling me. So what does that mean? Will she recognise you?'

'Most times, she knows who I am. It's not that severe yet. But she will forget things. You know, what she's done that day or yesterday or even last week or last month. She gets confused about things; sometimes she thinks I'm her brother and he died a lifetime ago. Some days I'll arrive and she will want to go for a walk but changes into her slippers. Once, I found her reading glasses in the mini-bar in her room and last time I visited, she just came back from a boat trip,' he said.

'That's nice, a day outing.'

'Trust me, she hasn't been on a boat anytime in the last twenty years!'

'Oh, I see,' I said.

Our hot drinks arrived and we thanked the waiter. I poured milk into my cup.

'Jason, how would you feel about maybe taking advantage of the situation; maybe try and encourage her to think you are your father? I know that's a bit unscrupulous but if it doesn't cause her too much pain and gives you a result ...'

'You mean, encourage the dialogue and see if it leads to any insights or confessions,' he stirred his second cappuccino.

'Yes.'

'I'm ahead of you. I've been trying to get that happening for a while.'

'Oh, good,' I said surprised.

He read my reaction. 'I didn't tell you because ...'

'You were hoping I would be a good enough detective to come up with it by myself?'

'No,' he laughed. 'I didn't want you to think I was, I don't know, unscrupulous as you said!'

'Never!' I said. 'So in the past, has she revealed anything?'

'Not really and I haven't pushed too hard. On one hand, I don't want to upset her unnecessarily, but on the other hand, if she was a part of Mom's demise, I don't care if she's my last relative on this earth or how old and frail she's become, I want to know.'

'OK, well let's do it and do it with a bit of sensitivity. We'll think of some leading questions and work them into your dialogue with her.'

'It's bizarre,' he looked outside at the passers-by, 'to think sugar could have killed my mother. To think it could be that simplistic.'

'It's pretty complicated. To train the immune system to reject something ...'

'I wish I could have done something,' he continued, 'if I had been a little bit older and could have talked with Mom or taken her seriously when she told me .... Why didn't I tell someone?' He looked at me his face full of anxiety.

'You did, Jason, you told your father your fears. You were six years old. Your entire world consists of your parents. Who else would you tell? Who would believe you? If a six-year-old told me his mother was being poisoned and I found out she was sick, under the care of a doctor and her husband was a pharmacist, I would feel pretty safe that she was in good hands!'

He sighed. 'Yeah, you are right. I'm just ...' He searched for the word.

'Frustrated?'

He looked straight at me. 'Angry ... guilty ... helpless,' he fired the words.

'When can we go to the nursing home?' I asked.

'Weekends are best, but does that suit you?'

'That's no problem.'

'OK. Saturday 11am?' Jason asked.

'Done,' I wrote it in my diary.

Chapter 16

I STOOD IN THE lounge room with the lights off, looking out the window. Atlas stood beside me looking as well; I suspect we were looking for different things. I couldn't see any headlights; it didn't appear anyone had followed me home. I was a little freaked out and jumped about three feet when I felt a hand on my shoulder.

'What's wrong?' Dom had exited the shower and come up behind me.

'There was a letter on my car window when I got in ...'

'Why didn't you call me?' he snapped.

'Dom, you can't be there every minute of the day. I just wanted to get home before it got too late. It may be nothing; we can open it now.'

'I want you to give this investigator stuff up. You don't need it, Jesse, just let it go and go back to the publicity business with Ed.'

'I'm not giving it up and ...'

He cut me off. 'Why would you put yourself in danger? Haven't you got anything to live for?'

I was beginning to see red. 'Dom, why does this always come back to you? I'm not giving it up, so get over it.'

'Well, maybe I don't want to,' he retorted.

'That's your choice. Do I ever ask you to give up anything?'

'No,' he agreed, 'but if you did, I would consider it.'

'Really?' I asked. 'Well if I said your profession was making me insecure, you are surrounded by beautiful women all the time, why can't you just do lecturing work, would you?'

Dom scoffed at me. 'First of all, I know you don't feel like that, and second, if you did, it's not the same thing. I'm not in danger of being bumped off by a beautiful woman in lycra.'

He had a point.

'Listen,' I gathered myself, 'let's just read the letter. It may be nothing.'

'I'll open it, just in case,' heroically, he moved toward the letter.

'No, you won't. This is my job, my responsibility.'

Dom picked the letter up off the table. 'We're not fighting about this, Jesse; I'm opening it.' And with that, he broke the seal and opened the envelope. He pulled out a single sheet of paper, looked inside the envelope, found nothing and handed it to me.

I took it from him and opened the letter. A message was scribbled in black pen, and I read it aloud.

Drop the case. Tell Renzo that there's no evidence and let it go.

I looked at both sides of the paper.

'That's it,' I told Dom.

'Then drop it. Whoever wrote it is right, drop it.'

'I saw someone in the car park at work – just for a minute, someone moving behind my car,' I thought aloud.

'Who was it?' Dom asked.

'I don't know. I saw them out of the corner of my eye, turned back and they were gone. They must have been putting the letter on the car window.'

'Did it look like Vince?' Dom asked.

'I honestly can't say. It was a blur.'

Dom sat on the edge of the dining room table and pulled me between his legs. He only had a towel on, and I was still in my sweaty running gear.

'Please, Jesse,' he kissed me on the lips. 'Give it up.'

I pulled back. 'I'm still stinky, and you're not,' I stated the obvious.

'Tell me you'll give it up.'

'Let me have a shower, and I'll think about it.'

He sighed with relief.

'I'm thinking about it, not doing it,' I reminded him.

'It's a start,' he smiled. 'I'll open a bottle of wine.'

'Yes, please.' As Dom rose, I grabbed the towel around his waist and headed up the stairs.

·ᐧ·ᐧ·

I stepped into the shower and thought about the letter. Would Vince have written it, or perhaps Yvonne? Maybe it's not connected to them. There was something that still bugged me about the whole Ren case. Something that didn't add up. My gut instinct said that Vince didn't do it. He had spent his life in Ren's shadow. Would Ren hitting on his girl be enough to push him over the edge? Why didn't he confront Ren? Challenge him to a fight? Blowing up his car may be an eye for an eye, but if Ren doesn't know who did it, does Vince get any satisfaction? It just wasn't sitting well with me.

I heard Dom yell from downstairs. I hated that. I used to do the same thing when I was a kid, and my mother used to go mad at me for yelling. A few minutes later, his head appeared around the bathroom door. 'How long are you going to be in there? I thought you might need help.'

I turned off the taps, and Dom passed me a towel as I stepped out of the shower.

'I was just washing away the day.'

'Hungry?' he asked.

'I could eat.'

'Let's eat later then,' Dom suggested.

'So what do you want to do now?' I asked, knowing full well. 'Haven't you got a lecture to prepare for?'

'I was going to show you my etchings first,' he teased.

He wrapped his arms around me and picked me up, towel and all.

'You know,' I said as we headed for the bedroom, 'now that you have moved in, it doesn't mean you get sex every time you see me like you did when we lived apart.'

'Doesn't it?' he looked disappointed. 'Can we negotiate?'

He dropped me on the bed and lowered himself on top of me. I loved it when he did that, and I could see the muscles flex in his arms. A negotiation was a very good idea.

I woke up; it was still dark. I could hear Dom breathing steadily beside me. I turned to see the digital clock, and it read 3:43am. Ren woke me up – he was in my head. Why was he alone in the café that morning? Who was he supposed to be meeting? He wouldn't have met Vince because he was living with him then. Now that I knew him better, he didn't seem like the type to go to breakfast or for a coffee alone. How come he didn't have someone sleeping over? He was the stallion, after all. Did he go to this coffee shop routinely, and did someone know his movements? I went there regularly and didn't recognise him, but I didn't go at the same time every week, and he might not have either.

The more I thought about it, the more I realised it was odd. I remember him saying what he had for breakfast, but was he waiting for someone? Had they stood him up? If Ren was going to meet someone, could this person, man or woman, be involved? That would make sense with the letter, the fear that I would not let the case go. Why wouldn't Ren tell me if he was meeting someone? Unless he didn't want me to know … unless he was there alone … I went around in circles.

I looked at the clock again; it was 3.55am. *Go back to sleep*, I told myself. The alarm would not buzz for another few hours yet.

⸻ ℓℓℓ ⸻

I dropped in to see Ren at his apartment at 9am. I figured he wouldn't start work until closer to the lunch shift. I didn't want to talk with him over the phone in case he fobbed me off while he came up with an answer; I wanted to read his reaction.

He was surprised to see me but pleased, assuming I had some information on his case. He invited me in and I had to give him credit, he looked pretty good with bed hair and a tracksuit on. Not as good as Dominic, though.

'Is Vince here?' I asked him.

'No,' he grabbed two coffee mugs. 'He starts work at eight. He's long gone.'

'Where does he work?'

'He's an auto electrician. He works at a place called Autolec. Know it?'

As if.

'No,' I answered. 'Has he been there long?'

'Forever. He did his apprenticeship there and eventually bought into the business. He and the old guy run it and get on like a house on fire. Vince runs the joint, and the old man keeps out his hair. They do nicely out of it, and both are happy with the arrangement.'

I nodded.

'So what's up?' he asked, sitting opposite me and putting the coffees on the two coasters on the glass table. He was well-trained.

'Sorry, I just dropped in unannounced, but I was going to see a client when something occurred to me.' I looked at him. 'Who were you meeting with that morning at the coffee shop before your car blew up?'

Ren stopped moving. He looked away and back again –
a telltale sign that he was just about to lie. 'Uh, no one, I
just stopped in for breakfast.'

'On your own?'

'Sure, why not?'

'Who were you meeting?' I asked again.

'Jeez, you are like the cops. I've hired you, remember, to
ask the questions, not give me the third degree.'

'I know. But all my questions lead me back to this one.
What's the big deal, tell me?'

'No big deal. What difference does it make?' he asked.

'Because whoever was supposed to meet you knew you
were there, so could have planned for this to happen given
they knew your whereabouts.'

'I doubt he'd do that,' he scoffed.

'Why?'

He realised he had admitted there was a possible
someone.

'I mean, I doubt it was that planned, whoever did it ...
assuming it was a guy,' he stumbled.

'Why?'

'Because ...'

'Vince was the last person to ring you on your phone,' I told
him. 'He obviously wasn't meeting you since he lived with you,
and you would have gone to the café together. Was he ringing

to tell you someone wasn't arriving? Someone who had called your apartment after you left, maybe?' I kept pushing him.

'Slow down, slow down,' he said, putting his thumbs on his temple. 'Let me think a minute. I didn't get to speak to Vince, you know that, I told you the car blew up and I didn't know who called.'

I nodded my agreement. 'Yep, we covered that,' I knew he was stalling. 'But?'

'But what?' he asked. He looked genuinely confused. I think I had talked him around in a circle; he wasn't that bright.

'No problem. Vince will tell me why he was calling you, and there's always your home phone record,' I concluded.

'Are you investigating me now?' he said with rising anger.

'No. But if there are grounds to do so, I will pass my information to the police.' I realised I was in a dangerous situation to be making these kinds of threats, alone in his apartment with him.

'You are a piece of work,' he shook his head.

'Did you want me to find who did it or just want me to fluff around and get a result for your insurance claim?'

'Fine. I was supposed to meet a girl for breakfast, and she didn't show.'

'But you said before that it was a 'he'.'

'I meant 'she'.'

'So what's the big deal, why couldn't you tell me that?' I looked at him, surprised.

'When was the last time you boasted about being stood up?'

Good grief! I'm an idiot. I should have realised his ego may have been at stake and I went about it the wrong way.

'Her loss,' I said, trying to sound casual. I noticed a glimmer of a smile.

'So, have you spoken to her since? Any idea why she didn't show?'

'She rang Vince and said something had come up. Vince rang to tell me but didn't get the message to me, as you know.'

'Why didn't she call you on your mobile phone? Did she have that number?'

'Yes. I don't know why she didn't call that number. Maybe she accidentally dialled the home number first. Maybe she hoped to catch me before I left home to save me from going out.'

'What is her name?' I got out my notepad and pen.

'Are you going to contact her?'

'I'm going to investigate her,' I told him. 'Don't you want me to?'

He thought about it for a minute. 'Yeah, stuff her. Why not? Her name is Melanie. Melanie Davies.'

My Melanie!

'Melanie Davies,' I repeated the name. 'My friend, Melanie who you took to dinner?'

He stared at me. 'Oh, I forgot that she was your pal.'

I sighed. 'Melanie wouldn't want to blow you up. She barely knows you and didn't know you then, nor did I! I introduced you after the bombing.'

'Oh yeah,' he looked away.

I rose. 'Thanks for the coffee. I'll come back to you if I have any other great insights.'

'Yeah, thanks, you are doing a great job. So what's your next lead?'

'I'm going to talk to Vince and ask who called you that morning.'

Ren jumped to his feet. 'Just drop it,' he said. 'Just drop the case. It's not important anymore.'

'Good, I'll send you my bill.'

'OK,' he agreed. That wiped the smile from his face. I waited until I got in the lift and groaned aloud with frustration. Ren was doing my head in.

As soon as I left the lift downstairs, I grabbed my phone and called Vince. As expected, the line was engaged. *Funny that.* I bet Ren could hardly wait for me to leave so he could call Vince to get him to collaborate his story. Didn't Ren think I would also collaborate it with his phone records? The guy was an idiot.

Ren didn't know I had spoken with Vince before arriving at his apartment. Wait until Vince told him that; I wish I were there to see that reaction. I knew who Ren was supposed to meet that morning. Ren would have to get up earlier in the morning to pull one over me.

Chapter 17

Roberto Altino was a beautiful man; model material; square jaw, a trendy stubble on his face, deep-brown eyes and black hair, short at the sides and back, with long strands swept back from his eyes. He wore cream pleated pants that looked like they were from the twenties, a black wool jumper with a cream neckband and black patent leather shoes. He didn't look overtly gay, and his mannerisms were not gay, but was he in love with Renzo Leonardo?

I pulled my car into a car park near the men's boutique where Roberto worked. It was in an up-market part of town where all the fashion boutiques boasted designer labels and exclusive garments. Walking by the store's glass windows, I could see Roberto attending to a customer. I entered and milled around in the background while he completed the transaction. He sold a shirt, a pair of pants and a tie for $650. Not bad. He acknowledged me with a nod. I noticed the gold wedding band on his finger and wondered who the lucky Mrs Altino was and whether she really existed.

He saw the customer out and turned to greet me.

'You must be Jesse?' he looked me up and down. I hope I was worthy.

'I am, and you must be Roberto?' I shook his hand and gave him my business card. 'Thank you for seeing me.'

'Pleasure,' he said in a sexy Italian accent. He looked at my card and then back at me. 'This is about Renzo?'

'It is.'

He shook his head. 'Ah, Renzo.'

'Can I be direct?' I asked.

Roberto smiled. He looked around. 'It is just you and me here, by all means.'

'How long have you and Ren been seeing each other?'

Roberto's cheeks puffed as he exhaled. 'That is direct.'

I nodded. He stalled. *He must be contemplating whether to deny it*, I thought.

Then, he told the truth. 'Before I answer, I need to tell you that my wife doesn't know I am in a relationship with Ren; she believes we are friends.'

'I understand,' I said.

'And I will deny the relationship if you tell her,' he continued.

'There is no need to tell her unless you are going to jail for the attempted murder of Renzo; then she may know.'

He laughed. 'No. Renzo is an egomaniac, arrogant and stupid sometimes, but I do care for him enough not to want to kill him.'

'So, how long have you been seeing each other?' I asked again.

'Eight months and two weeks.'

Wow, that must be love, I thought. *I've been seeing Dom for ... hmm, I would have to work it out.* I continued questioning Roberto.

'And you had a falling out?'

'You could say that,' Roberto's face dropped. 'We broke up several weeks ago.'

'Can I ask why?' I studied him. He looked upset. 'It may help me understand Ren and his case better,' I explained.

'And to work out if I'm a suspect?' Roberto's turn to be blunt.

'Maybe,' I agreed.

'Are you seeing him?' Roberto asked.

'Who?' I was a bit confused.

'Ren?'

'No. No, definitely not,' I assured him. 'I live with my partner; we've been together for a few years.' It's a good thing I started on that math equation earlier!

'Doesn't seem to matter these days whether people have a partner or not,' he sounded bitter. 'Everyone cheats.'

'Is that why you broke up? Was Ren cheating on you?' I glanced at his wedding ring as I said this, and he noticed.

'I got married young, in my early twenties. It was the desire of both of our parents ... it's a cultural thing ... two strong Italian families ... Catholics ...' his voice faded.

I didn't say anything, waiting for him to continue.

'She is a lovely lady. We have two children; she is a good wife and mother.'

'But you are in love with Ren,' I said.

'I was,' he snapped, 'but he can't be loyal. I guess that sounds strange, given that I'm cheating, but I don't play the field. She is my wife, and he is my lover. I'm not cheating on her with another woman or on him with another man.'

Big deal, some consolation to his wife!

Roberto continued. 'Whereas Ren doesn't know if he wants a girlfriend or boyfriend. He's playing in both fields.'

'So what happened on that Sunday morning when you were supposed to meet him for brunch?'

He looked surprised.

'Vince told me that you called to cancel,' I tittle-tattled.

'Hmm, Vince. So, did Ren send you here to ask me these questions?' Roberto frowned. He moved to a table of wool knit sweaters and refolded them.

'No, Ren doesn't know that I know you were meeting for brunch.' I sighed and elaborated. 'Ren has hired me to find out who blew up his car, but he has only given me half the story. I keep turning up things, and whether Ren likes them or not, I have to explore these options. At the end of the day, he is paying me to get results. Did you blow up his car?'

Roberto looked up and then laughed.

'No. But I wish I had. I'm only joking. I didn't blow up his car. There's only one thing of Ren's I want to blow.'

I grimaced.

'I apologise. I get crude when I get angry and frustrated.'

'That's OK,' I said, relieved that we weren't going to stay on that track. 'So why didn't you meet him for brunch?' I persisted.

Roberto moved to another rack and started straightening ties. 'Earlier that week, I discovered that he had sex with Vince's girlfriend. That was the final straw, so I called it off.'

I wanted to ask how he found out but didn't want to interrupt him.

Roberto continued. 'He wanted to get together that morning to talk about reconciling. I put him off a few times, but, in all honesty, I was missing him. I agreed to meet him for brunch. I told my wife I was going to the gym, but she got called into work, and I had to cancel with Ren or bring the children. I tried to call him to cancel, but he'd already left for the cafe. I think I woke Vince up. You know he's staying with Ren at the moment?'

I nodded. 'I know.'

Roberto continued. 'Anyway, Vince said he had to give Ren another message so he would call him right away and let him know. That suited me, my wife was in the other room getting dressed and if she heard me, she would want to know who I was calling at that hour of the morning.'

What other message did Vince give Ren? I stored that away.

'Do you have any idea who may want to hurt Ren or his car?' I continued.

Roberto seemed to give the question serious consideration. 'No. I imagine Ren has hurt a lot of people over the years, lovers mainly, but blowing up cars is not just a male crime, is it?'

His question threw me. I thought back to my studies. 'Well, yes, normally it is. Anything to do with bombs is usually male-skewed.'

The door to the store opened, and two young men walked in.

'I have to go,' Roberto said.

'Of course, and thank you for your time,' I headed for the door and thought of something else. 'Roberto, just one last, quick question ...'

He waited, eyebrows raised.

'How did you meet Ren?'

'Through Vince. Vince's girlfriend or ex-girlfriend, Yvonne, is my wife's sister.'

My mouth dropped open. I was thinking aloud. 'Sorry ... so Yvonne is your sister-in-law?'

'Yes. Nice girl,' he smiled and went to serve the two young men.

I headed into the chilly air. So, Vince, Yvonne, and Roberto are all connected: a wife who might know her husband is cheating with Ren, a best friend who knows Ren has cheated with his girlfriend, that same girlfriend who is pregnant with Ren's child and two women who are sisters and have been mistreated by Ren. I had gone from having no one with a grudge against Ren to a line of people. I was beginning to want to blow him up myself!

Chapter 18

THE NURSING HOME WAS buried in suburbia, fenced off from the rest of the neighbourhood by a concrete wall painted in a port wine colour. It was a calling card for graffiti artists, and I was surprised they had been restrained to date. The only identifying feature was a small sign on the external wall near the driveway entrance. It read 'Green Burrows Home'. I looked around but couldn't see too many green burrows. At least the name didn't offer too many false promises. I remember when my grandmother was in the last years of her life and living at a nursing home called 'Hopetown'. It was evident after one visit that residents only hoped to go to a better place.

I agreed to meet Jason at the bench in the garden. I sat on the bench and wondered why I didn't wait in the car; it was freezing, so I stuck my hands in my black wool coat pockets. Another car pulled up, and a middle-aged couple got out. We greeted each other as they passed. It was visiting hours, so I expected some traffic at the home. A white four-wheel drive swung into the driveway and pulled into the nearest car park. Jason jumped out and strode towards me. He was wearing jeans and a red bomber jacket.

'Sorry I'm late.'

'You're fine, I'm early,' I told him. I indicated the bench, and he sat down.

'Before we go in, let's review our strategy. I'm going to be your girlfriend who you have brought in to meet Esme, unless she identifies me as someone else before you do the introduction.'

'Agreed,' he said.

'We'll just throw in a few leading questions about your parents, particularly your father – you know, talk about our love and ask about hers – see where it leads us.'

'Yep, no problem,' he rubbed his hands together from the cold or nervousness.

'Then, if nothing turns up, which is likely given you have already tried this a few times,' I warned him, 'then next time, I suggest you visit in some of your dad's clothing, something she may recognise. You don't look much like him, but we could do wonders with some Brylcreem and a costume change,' I teased him.

He smiled. 'Brylcreem ... I remember Dad using that!'

'Mine too! Ready?' I stood up.

'Yep,' he rose, and we walked to the front stairs. He held the door open for me. We walked down the tiled floors, and I couldn't help but look at each room as we passed. Rows and rows of elderly folk; some sleeping, some watching television, some speaking with visiting relatives. Maybe those with dementia are the lucky ones – able to escape somewhere in their mind or dreams – rather than waiting in the twilight zone. But that's easy to say when you are in your thirties.

Jason stopped at a room on my left and tapped on the door. He smiled. I could tell he had a genuine affection for his aunt.

I glanced in from behind him. She was a tiny woman with white hair that made her look older than her years; I would have put her in her eighties, not seventies. She sat upright in a chair near the window and wore a pale blue dress with a white knitted cardigan over the top. Around her neck was a string of cream pearls, and several large diamond rings were on her index finger.

'Hello, Aunt Esme,' he winced and glanced at me; he had forgotten the game plan and called her Aunt.

She clapped her hands together.

'Jason,' she said, 'how lovely of you to come.'

He leaned over and kissed her on the cheek. From the photos, she looked a little like her sister, Isabella, with fine cheekbones, pale skin and sharp, blue eyes. I looked back at

Jason. He also inherited features from his mother's side of the family.

'And you have brought a friend ...' Esme continued.

'Yes, Aunt, this is Jesse,' Jason introduced me.

'I knew a Jesse once,' she smiled, 'but he was a man and a handsome one at that. But these days, the names are all mixed up, aren't they? Where are my manners? Please, please take a seat.'

I thanked her and looked around. There were two brown vinyl chairs in the corner. Jason grabbed both and moved them closer.

'Now, Jason, is this your girlfriend?' she turned to me and continued without waiting for an answer, 'I am always telling Jason he needs to get out and meet a lovely girl, get married and have children. He's an only child and he must carry on his family name. Will you two get married?' she asked.

Jason fidgeted, embarrassed; I thought it was amusing.

'We may yet,' I teased him, 'if he sweeps me off my feet,' I told Esme.

She laughed. 'Good for you, dear. We should have tea, but getting service in this hotel is always difficult.'

Jason glanced at me again. I didn't correct her; it was much nicer to believe you were in a hotel than a hostel.

'There's a kettle here, Aunt, I'll make tea for the three of us, it will be quicker than room service.' Jason rose and filled the kettle at the hand basin.

I glanced out the window.

'You have a lovely view,' I took in the centre square with the large tree dominating the view and the white wrought iron bench underneath. An elderly gentleman sat there with a crochet rug on his lap.

Esme looked out, saw the man, looked away and back again.

'It is a lovely view,' she agreed. 'I like to sit here. Jason's father likes it, too. He loves that tree. I'm always telling him to come back inside; it's too cold, but he loves to sit there.'

I looked again and followed her gaze; she was looking at the elderly gentleman under the tree and calling him Jason's father. Jason frowned and leaned over to look out.

'Aunt, you know my father has ... you remember he died,' he struggled with the words.

Esme ignored him. 'He'll catch a cold.'

The kettle boiled and made a shrill sound, breaking our concentration.

'White with none, Jesse?' he asked.

'Yes, please, I'm amazed you remembered.'

Jason smiled. 'And for you, Aunt, white with two sugars.'

She turned sharply and looked at him.

'You know I like to put my own sugar in, thank you, Charles.'

'Are you OK?' I asked Jason as we headed to our cars. He was upset and distracted. Esme was tired after her tea, and we left soon afterward.

'Maybe I should just let this go,' he said, 'it's just causing me more grief.' He ran his hand over his mouth and leaned back to sit on the bonnet of his car. 'But then I'll never know.'

'I guess you have to weigh up which will cause you the most concern: digging up skeletons or not taking this opportunity to find the truth while you have the chance ... while Esme is still with us.'

He looked like he needed someone to hold him, and if I were a single girl, I would have jumped at the chance. In my current situation, it was just inviting trouble.

'Do you want to go somewhere and have a coffee and talk?' I offered, hoping he would say no, as Dom had the day off, and it was Saturday.

He shook his head. 'Thanks, Jesse, but I'll be on duty for two hours. I have to get home and change. Thanks for coming with me.'

'I think we should visit again soon, maybe next week,' I told him. 'We had an insight today.'

'An insight! That's an understatement,' he exhaled, 'it freaked me out. Her reaction to the sugar and calling me by my father's name smacked of guilt. Why did she insist on putting her own sugar in? Didn't she trust Dad? Is that how he killed Mom, breaking down her system with the sugar? Does Esme know that?'

'Have you ever thought of just asking Esme if your father killed your mother?' I said in a low voice.

'Yes. But I thought if she had a heart attack because of my question, I wouldn't be able to live with myself. I would be my father's son; he kills Mom, I kill her sister.' He looked around the car park to see if anyone had heard him. 'I don't know whether to continue or not.'

'It's your call, Jason,' I said. 'You don't have to make a decision now. Let me know during the week, and whatever you decide to do is fine by me.'

'I will.' He squeezed my shoulder, 'Thanks.'

He opened his car door, and I turned to go to my car.

No more work or thinking about work for the rest of the day. I coached myself. *Maybe.*

I avoided the temptation to call in at the office and went straight home. I opened the garage door to drive in; Dom's car was missing. I reached for my phone.

'Hey, where are you?' I asked.

'Home.'

'Me too, but you're not here.'

'I'm here,' Dom answered. 'You're not here.'

'I'm here, in the garage.'

'Well, come inside,' he sounded surprised.

'But where's your car?'

There was a silence on the other end of the line. 'What do you mean?'

'It's not in the garage,' I told him. Again, the silence.

'Oh, that's right,' he sounded relieved, 'I loaned the car to Atlas. He's taken a girl Boxer out. She's a real bitch. No, it's getting serviced,' he finally informed me.

'You are a funny guy,' I told him. 'If I were you, I would hide now because I'm coming to get you.'

'Ooh, big scary detective,' the line dropped out.

Chapter 19

Green Burrows Nursing Home was easier to find the second time around. That wasn't always the case for me; I had no sense of direction. I grabbed the box of assorted chocolates from the car seat and headed inside, out of the cold. I wondered if Esme would remember me. There was a new batch of visitors' faces today. I greeted one of the nurses as I passed down the hallway and glanced into each room. I couldn't remember Esme's room, but I knew it was well along the hallway. I found the room, but it was empty. I checked the name on the door, and it was the right room. My first thought was that she had died; it was a bit dramatic, but you never know. I came back into the hallway, and a different nurse caught my eye this time.

'Mrs Abingdon will be back in a minute. She's having her hair cut, but she's almost done.'

'Thank you. Is it OK if I wait in here?' I indicated Esme's room.

'Of course,' the nurse said.

Mrs Abingdon, the second, I mused. I looked at my hair in the mirror in Esme's room. *I need a haircut, too. I guess the hairdresser comes on-site and does everyone over a few days. Good service.*

I sat in Esme's seat, looking out the window to the green square; no one sat under the tree this time. I thought about my strategy; I would tell Esme that I was seeing a client in the area, and I thought I would drop in. We could talk about Jason, I could fake how much I liked him and hoped to have his babies, maybe, and see where it led to. Jason was OK with the plan.

I had been sitting there for maybe ten minutes when I heard a nurse talking to a patient as they came down the hall. I rose and stuck my head out of the room; it was Esme returning.

'You have a visitor,' the nurse announced.

Esme looked up, surprised. She looked attractive for her age in that quaint way that some elderly people do. Well-groomed, well-dressed and with those pearls around her neck again.

She looked delighted to see me. 'Merle!' she announced. 'I thought you were abroad!'

'Hello!' I answered. I had no idea who Merle was but I may as well play along. 'You look lovely, Esme.'

'I've had my hair done,' she confirmed.

'Ah-ha, I knew there was something different. Well, it's just lovely.'

I followed her into the room, and the nurse waved as she left.

'I've brought you some chocolates,' I offered the box. 'Will I put the kettle on?'

'Ooh, delicious, thank you, you shouldn't have,' she smiled, taking the box and sitting in her customary chair. 'Yes, let's have a cup of tea and a chocolate. No nut ones, I hope.'

'No. I remembered you don't like the nut ones.' I congratulated myself for picking soft centres. 'I can't remember, what is your favourite?' I frowned.

'Turkish delight,' she answered without hesitation. 'Charles' favourite, too. We always fight over them. He'll be here soon; perhaps you better make three cups of tea.'

'I will,' I agreed. I decided to take a risk. 'Will Isabella be joining us?'

She looked confused, and then she answered.

'She's not well, dear, remember?'

'Yes, yes, of course. My mind is slipping these days. I'm so forgetful it is a wonder I don't go out with my slippers on,' I shook my head.

Esme laughed. 'Don't worry, Merle, it happens to all of us. How is Teddy?'

Lord knows how Teddy was, and I wanted to get the conversation back to Isabella.

'You know Teddy! Same as always,' I said.

She nodded and then smiled. 'He was always too smooth for his own good, that man of yours.'

'Yes indeed,' I agreed. 'But loveable.' *Teddy, you rogue!* I thought.

Esme laughed. She looked out the window.

I braced myself. 'Shall I put in milk and sugar?' I asked.

'Yes, two sugars, please,' she responded without hesitation. *Hmm, clearly it is only Charles she doesn't want to add her sugar.*

'So what has the doctor said about Isabella? Is there anything I can do?' I asked her.

Esme shook her head. 'Terrible state of affairs.' She took the cup of tea I handed her. 'It's taking its toll on Charles,' she sighed. 'Poor, poor, Charles. Isabella doesn't know how lucky she is to have him.' She opened the box of chocolates and looked at them. I picked up the chocolate box lid.

'I think that one is the Turkish delight,' I pointed.

She smiled and reached for it. She took a sample bite.

'Oh yes,' she savoured it.

'Does Jason realise how ill his mother is?' I continued.

'No, the dear little boy. I don't know what is going on with that lad, and Isabella is filling his head with silly ideas about being poisoned,' she made a tutting sound. 'I have told Isabella she need not worry. That boy will be cared for while I have breath in my body. He will always have a family; I will be there for him if anything happens to her.'

At least she genuinely did love Jason.

'Will she die?' I lowered my voice and sounded concerned.

'Yes, it is only a matter of time,' she shook her head. 'Charles is taking care of her. Poor, poor Charles. Isabella doesn't know how lucky she is,' she said again.

Poor Charles indeed! My mind was racing a hundred miles an hour. *How do I move this conversation forward?*

'Do you think she should be in the hospital?' I asked.

'Good Lord, no. They won't care for her like we will. Charles thinks she has an allergy, an intolerance, he calls it. She seems to be rejecting food that she always used to eat. Growing up, she had such a sweet tooth; we both did, but she never put on weight. I used to put on weight watching her eat,' Esme sighed at the memory. 'But now, she can't tolerate anything sweet.'

'Really?' I said. *Was Esme ensuring people knew Isabella had an 'allergy'?*

I could feel the vibration from the small tape recorder whirring away in my pocket. I would play it back to Jason and see what he thought. I kept the conversation flowing. 'I wish I could eat anything I like, but you know me, it goes straight to my hips. Anything with sugar ... I've such a sweet tooth ...'

It was an hour after Dom's last class, and there was no sign of him; he didn't answer his phone. My mind drifted to the worst-case scenarios – an accident at work or on his way home – or even worse, Dom was out with one of his gym bunny students. I could see some lithe blonde wearing lycra, battering her eyelashes at him and saying things like, 'Dom, you are so big and strong.' OK, maybe not quite that cliché. I rang reception at the gym and was told he left forty minutes ago; now I was worried.

Fifteen minutes later, the front door opened, and Dom walked in.

'Hi,' I called from the kitchen, 'I was worried about you, you're phone is off.'

'Sorry,' he called. 'Just got held up with a client. I'm going to have a shower; back in a minute.'

I came out of the kitchen, and he was gone. I didn't like this one bit. He walks in the door and goes straight to the shower. What had he been doing? I went up the stairs; my heart was feeling heavy. I knew we shouldn't have moved in together. I should have gone with my gut instinct. The bathroom door was closed, and the shower wasn't running. We rarely closed the bathroom door. It was quiet in there.

I knocked on the door. 'Can I come in?'

'No. Um, I'll just be a minute,' Dom said.

'What's going on?'

'Nothing,' Dom snapped. His voice softened. 'I'll be downstairs in a minute.'

I stood looking at the door. Something was wrong. No hello-kiss, no hug, straight to the bathroom, Dom snapping. I turned to go downstairs but stopped. I didn't know whether to barge into the bathroom or return to the kitchen. If he had been cheating, I would rather just find out now, get it over with and be alone. *Why did I let him move in? It was stupid. He works in the health industry; he's surrounded by beautiful women all the time. Did I really think he would stay with me and wouldn't be swayed?*

Dom must have thought I had gone back downstairs; the bathroom door opened, and he walked to the cupboard, opened it and grabbed a new towel, a navy towel. As he turned, I saw his face, and he saw me at the same time. My mouth dropped open, and I'm sure my eyes were huge. He had blood running down the side of his face, blood smeared across his cheek from where he had tried to stop his nose from bleeding and purple swelling around one eye.

'Jesse,' he said, startled.

'Dom, what happened?' I ran to him.

'Nothing,' he grabbed the towel and dodged me as he went back into the bathroom. I followed him in and found blood stains on the basin and the cream towel smeared with blood.

'Dom!'

'It's OK, Jesse, don't panic. Just give me a minute to clean up, and I'll be downstairs.'

I must have stood frozen because he stopped dabbing his face and turned to me.

'What happened?' I asked.

Dom shrugged. 'Just a boy's fight.'

'You're a man. Tell me!'

Dom sighed. 'I got mugged in the car park.'

'Did you call the police?'

'No.'

'I'm going to call Jason, Officer Abingdon,' I started out of the bathroom, but Dom grabbed my arm.

'Jesse, leave it.'

'Why? Why should I leave it?'

'It's not what you think.'

'I'm thinking you were mugged. Should I be thinking something worse?' I leaned past him, wet a hand towel, and dabbed at his face. He sat on the basin's edge. 'Did you hit on someone, and their partner beat you up? Did you come to the rescue of someone and get caught in the crossfire? Have you started boxing classes?'

Dom looked at me. 'I didn't hit on anyone or rescue anyone, and I do regular boxing classes. I sensed someone was following me in the car par,k and I was right. I turned around, this guy was there and he asked if I could give him directions. I knew

I was stitched then. I looked around and spotted the second one. I put up a pretty good fight, and they didn't get what they wanted – the car keys or my wallet.'

He winced as I dabbed antiseptic onto the cut above his eyebrow.

'I'm sorry, Dom,' I stopped and looked at him.

His face relaxed.

'I'll live.'

'You won't be quite as handsome for a while,' I teased him as I finished cleaning his wounds. 'Maybe you can sleep in the second room until then.'

He laughed. 'You don't have a second room.'

'Oh, that's right!'

'I'll just look butch for a while,' he assured me.

'As long as people don't think I did this to you,' I continued, trying to lift his spirits.

'Unlikely. You can barely reach my head, shorty.'

I narrowed my eyes. 'You've already had one fight tonight, don't pick another. You may not be so lucky next time.'

He grinned and winced again as I touched the towel with antiseptic to the cut on his forehead.

I wondered if he was telling the truth or protecting me.

'So, who is Merle?' I pulled the teabags out of the pot and looked for somewhere to put them. The café always made their tea too strong.

'Merle?' Jason repeated. He sat opposite me in a booth. It was odd having coffee with a cop. Everyone who came into the cafe glanced at him and looked away. The closeness of the coffee shop to his work guaranteed a regular parade of uniforms through the door.

'Merle,' he said again and laughed. He sipped his flat white. 'Merle left this earth about five years ago; before that, she was around forever, always in our life.'

'Great, so now I'm the walking dead!'

'Merle was Esme's neighbour before Esme moved in with us. They played bowls and went to church together. From memory, Merle's husband passed away not long after Mom died. She stayed a widow, though.'

'That would be the smooth Teddy?'

Jason laughed again. 'Teddy! Yes, from what I can remember, he was a bit of a lady's man in his day.' Jason sat back and shook his head. 'So Esme thought you were Merle ... interesting.'

I gave him the tape.

'Have you got a tape recorder to listen to that on?' I nodded at the tape.

'Yep, no problem. Give me the rundown.'

I filled him in on my conversation with Esme. 'I'm hopeful that perhaps she didn't know anything about it, but given she let me put her sugar in, I'm sceptical,' I finished. 'Listen to the tape and see what you think.'

'It would be great if she didn't know about it,' Jason agreed. 'I can't understand how she could do that to her sister. Of course there could be years of systematic denial in there, too. They say that sometimes chronic liars begin to believe their own lies.'

'Dominic was mugged last night,' I dropped that fact into the conversation.

Jason looked up. 'Your guy? Is he alright?'

'Yes. Just a cut above his eye and a bit of bruising.'

'Where did it happen?'

'He said in the car park near his work at the Lifestyle Health Club – one asking for directions, the other coming up from behind.'

Jason made a scoffing sound. 'It happens more than you know, and the two-man sting is common. Dominic shouldn't have fought them, though. Just give them what they want – usually, money, jewellery, that sort of thing.'

'I hope that's all it was,' I said. 'Dom's six foot plus, pretty brave taking him on.'

'Safety in numbers. Do you think there's more to it?

I shrugged. 'I don't know. I received an anonymous letter telling me to drop Ren's case. I'm wondering whether this is part of the persuasion.'

'Did they say anything to Dom?'

'Nothing that he's admitting.'

'I'll drop in and see him this afternoon.'

'Really?'

'Yeah, I'm on patrol, so I'll just cruise by the gym.'

'That would be great, Jason, thanks. He may tell you more. He's probably putting on a brave face around me and holding out.'

'Men!' Jason teased.

'I couldn't have said it better,' I laughed. 'Now, back to your case. If it's OK with you, I would like to visit Esme a few more times to try to get a result. Are you OK with me assuming the role of her dead friends?'

'Sure, it seems harmless enough,' he answered.

'After that, you may have to decide whether to let it go or not – history is against you,' I sighed.

'I know.' He finished his coffee, and I saw him gaze out of the window as a couple of heavily tattooed young men wearing hooded pullovers passed; it was an occupational hazard. He returned his attention to me. 'I think we are nearly there, and I think Esme will close it for us. Can you keep going for a while?'

'Of course,' I assured him. 'I want a result as much as you and I want the same result, I'm just not sure that we will get what we want.'

We sat in silence for a few minutes.

'Jason, is there anyone else your mother may have confided in? Anyone who may have visited your mother while she was ill? Someone who could tell us if she said anything to them about being poisoned? I know she was bedridden, but do you remember anyone visiting the house? Did she have a close friend or a family member she spoke with in person or by phone besides her sister? There must have been someone she was close with.'

Jason thought about it. 'I don't know. Mom was a fifties bride. She didn't go to work as women do now, so her social network was limited to Dad and family. But let me think about it. She must have had visitors, especially from junior school but I was pretty young, I don't remember any names off the top of my head or anyone even visiting.'

'What school did she go to?' I asked.

'Our Lady of Lourdes College for girls,' he said. 'But again, that was in the fifties.'

'What was her maiden name?'

'Stewart.'

'I'll do some homework,' I told him. 'See if there are any school yearbooks or records, reunions planned, that sort of thing. If I can find some names or photos, it may just jar your memory.'

'Thanks, Jesse,' he brightened.

'Hey, it is all part of the service. Now, on another matter, I was hoping to get your help again.'

'Shoot,' he said. 'I mean that literally.'

I laughed. 'It's about Ren and his car bomb.' I filled Jason in on the Ren situation and the foursome – Vince, Ren's lover Roberto, Roberto's wife and Roberto's sister-in-law and ex-girlfriend of Vince – who all had a grudge and a motive against him.

'So he won't be winning any popularity awards this week?' Jason concluded.

'Safe to say,' I agreed. 'I was hoping you could help me close this one by leaning on them.'

'What did you have in mind?' he asked.

'I think all four of them are in it together. I don't know if there was enough anger there to kill him, I think they just wanted to teach him a lesson, make him think about his actions a little. So I was hoping we could bring Roberto and his wife into the station and that you could question them separately. I'll ensure Vince and Yvonne know Roberto and his wife are at the station, someone might cave in. What do you think?'

'Why those two, why not bring Vince and Yvonne in for questioning?' Jason asked.

'Because Vince is seasoned. I don't think he'll be easily intimidated in the presence of police or at the station. Yvonne might be, but she's been around him long enough to be a bit streetwise. I'm guessing this would be a new and somewhat frightening experience for Roberto and his wife.'

'Makes sense. Let me talk to my boss, see if it's OK with him, and I'll get back to you. I'm sure he'd like to mark a file closed and count it in his statistics.'

'Thanks for that,' I reached for my jacket and put it back on. 'I've got to run, and you should get back out there and keep the streets safe.'

He rolled his eyes and paid the bill.

Chapter 20

I COULD HEAR THE clock ticking on the wall. It chimed at 11.30, and then the silence returned. I stopped to listen to the quiet and sat momentarily, just being still. Ed was at a meeting and I was meeting-free. I thought about Dom; there was something odd about his mugging, how he didn't want to report it, and how he avoided my questions. But then again, perhaps that is how Dom reacts to these sorts of things. He had never been ill or hurt while we had been dating, so I had no benchmark.

I looked back at my computer screen and searched for school reunion websites. There were quite a few. I went into one, put in Isabella's name and maiden name, the school she attended, and her age as it would be now, and waited. I turned down several options to sign up, list my profile and receive monthly reports. Finally, the results came back. I could not believe it; five Isabella Stewarts had attended Our Lady of Lourdes College for girls in the fifties and sixties. I thought the records would not go back that far – I was wrong – there was plenty of interest in finding old school friends. I scrolled down the list. This was going to be harder than I thought. There was an Isabella Corrine Stewart, an Isabella Jane Stewart, an Isabella Mary Stewart, an Isabella Catherine Stewart and an Isabella Anne Stewart, all in the right age group. It was a good start.

I sent a message to Jason asking for his mother's middle name. In a matter of minutes, he sent back a text. Her middle name was Mary.

Got you, Isabella. Now, I've just got to find your friends!

⌒⌒⌒

'Good Lord, it's like a morgue in here,' Ed stormed into the office. I jumped a foot from fright.

'Gotcha!' he grinned. 'What's happening?'

'You scared the hell out of me.'

'Can't have you enjoying the peace and quiet can we?'

I looked Ed up and down. 'I feel like I haven't seen you for a week instead of a weekend.'

'Well, you can spend quality time with me sharing those publicity files any time you are ready to step back into your old stilettos.'

'Hmm, tempting,' I agreed.

'How are the two cases coming along?' Ed dropped into his chair and logged onto the computer.

'I'm about to put the squeeze on both, so I think there will be a result by the end of this week, and one way or the other, I'll be closing the files.'

'Ooh, sounds exciting,' Ed's eyes were huge. 'Speaking of which, did you meet with Mona of the choir on Friday?'

'I did. God bless, Mona. I finished a publicity strategy for her on the weekend and emailed it last night. I copied you in. When she signs off on it, I'll kick into action. How's your workload?'

'Good. The film got some good publicity in its first week of release, and the client was delighted with the opening week box office take. I thought the number of bums on seats was a bit ordinary, but it was a morose film. Anyway, we've scored their next film. The water campaign is also humming along. We're going into two different councils with the same campaign we did here, so it's really just a case of adjusting the advertisements and rebooking with the local papers. Last but not least, I've been with the fun run team this morning; two months until the big day, so we are about to launch the media campaign.'

'You're on fire!' I looked at my watch. It was almost midday already. 'Want to do lunch?'

'Is the Pope Catholic?' Ed asked. Just let me check my emails, and I will be right with you.'

I passed Ed the salt and told him about Dom getting bashed up. He choked on a chip.

'Is he alright?'

'Yes, but he won't report it. I think there's more to it.' I searched my salad for the avocado promised on the menu.

'He's a guy,' Ed reminded me. 'He's not going to run to the cops to say he got smacked and came off second best. Come on, Dom's probably been worked over a few times in his life; guys just take it.'

'Hmm, maybe you're right.' A text came through on my phone. I flipped it open. 'Excellent,' I looked up at Ed. 'It's from Jason. He got approval. Tomorrow morning, we can pick up two suspects in the Ren case and take them into the station for questioning.'

'Bully for you.' Ed raised his eyebrows, 'aren't we making friends in high places?'

'I need more friends in high places.'

Ed waved his fork at me, 'I have a friend who is an ex-cop and is now an ambulance officer.'

I must have looked confused as Ed elaborated.

'An ambulance officer has connections everywhere. I swear he knows things are going to happen before they do. I must introduce you to Jim.'

'That would be handy, thanks.'

'He'll do anything for a six-pack of beer.'

'Cheap and easy,' I said. 'Just as we like them.'

'Here, here, sister,' Ed raised his glass, and we clinked them.

Roberto Altino looked frightened, handsome, but frightened. He wore a navy wool jumper and jeans with brown leather shoes. His hair was slicked back, and he had a designer stubble across his face. His eyes darted around the room, and he fidgeted, wrung his hands, placed them flat on the table and then on his lap. He was obviously new to the police interrogation scene. I watched through the two-way glass as Jason entered the room where Roberto waited.

'Where's my wife?' Roberto asked.

Jason sat down. He opened a manila folder on the table and took a pen from his shirt pocket.

'I'm Officer Jason Abingdon. Your wife is fine. She is down the hallway talking with another member of our police team.'

'What about?'

'The same thing I am going to talk with you about, Renzo Leonardo's car bombing. Then I'm going to talk with Vince Palino and Yvonne Benedetto.'

Roberto didn't say anything. He leaned forward on the table.

Eventually, he spoke. 'Should I have a lawyer?' he asked.

'You are not under arrest. I just want to talk with you about the car bombing. Do you need a lawyer?'

He scoffed. 'Of course I don't.'

'You can call one if you want to,' Jason offered. 'We'll just make it a formal proceeding then, and I'll read you your rights and tape the session.'

'I don't need a lawyer. So if I'm not under arrest, I can leave anytime I like ... with my wife?' Roberto asked.

'Anytime you like,' Jason agreed. 'But then that will look suspicious,, so I'll probably have to read you your rights, and you may want to get a lawyer.'

Jason watched Roberto as he processed the information.

Jason continued. 'Just a few questions; I thought you could help us with our investigation.'

'How?' Roberto shot back.

Jason tapped the table with his fingers. 'Well if you stop asking me questions I can get to my questions.'

Roberto nodded.

'When did the three of you decide to teach Ren a lesson?' Jason delivered the question like a blow between the eyes, and Roberto reeled back.

Jason continued.

'Not that he didn't deserve it after playing around with your sister-in-law and his best friend's girlfriend ...'

Roberto's mouth opened, but he didn't say anything. His hands worked the edge of the table.

'Which of course meant your wife was going to find out,' Jason continued. 'Did you mean to harm him or just give him a scare?'

Roberto stumbled, his words tripping over each other. 'No ... neither ... we didn't. I didn't have anything to do with his car blowing up.'

'I would have blown him up, or at least his car, if it was me. Are you sure you weren't tempted to do the same?' Jason raised his eyebrows.

'Why would I want to do that? What's the point?' Roberto asked.

'He loves that car, doesn't he?'

Roberto shrugged.

'You love him. You love your wife. He took something from you, Vince and Yvonne, and in return, you all took one of his beloved prizes away from him.'

Roberto sat back and shook his head. 'No way. That's stupid.'

'Really? Does your wife know about you and Ren?'

'No.'

'Are you sure because she was pretty angry at him just now? It seemed she had a motive.'

'She knows about Yvonne and Ren. She's angry that her sister's been done over. You won't tell her ... about Ren and me?'

Jason looked down at his notes. 'It will come out during discussions. It is a motive, after all.'

'I want to see her now,' Roberto pushed his chair back and stood up.

'You will have to wait for her to come out of her interview,' Jason looked at his watch. 'I imagine she will only be a few minutes.'

'I need to see her!' Roberto headed for the door.

Jason stood. 'Wait here. I'll see if she's finished and bring her to you.'

Jason walked from the room. Roberto paced, ran his hands through his hair, grabbed his phone and went to call someone, then stopped. He exhaled, then continued dialling. The number must have gone to voicemail.

Roberto swore under his breath, 'Damn, Vince, where are you?'

He hung up and tried another number. There was no answer again, and he continued to swear. He was working himself into a state.

Jason joined me behind the glass, and we watched him for a while.

'I don't know whether he's freaking out about the crime or his wife finding out about him and Ren,' I turned to Jason.

'Yeah, hard to tell, but he called Vince first, not Ren. I'm going to have a few words with his wife. Want to come and watch?'

'Sure,' I said. I left the view of Roberto stewing and moved down the hallway, following Jason into the back entrance of another room.

'Is there any point reading Roberto his rights?' I asked Jason.

He shrugged. 'Not at this stage. Let's face it, even if they confess, it's unlikely that Ren will press charges against his best friend, the woman expecting his baby and his lover. But if Roberto's wife gives up any secrets, I will read Roberto his rights just for good measure before he admits to anything.'

'Good luck,' I said as Jason pointed me to the door and exited the room.

'Thanks,' he said.

I went up to the glass and could see an attractive woman of European descent. She had wavy hair, blow-dried to perfection, large dark eyes and a petite face. A sufficient cleavage peeked from a modest, fitted grey top. She was sophisticated, a good match for Roberto and more glamorous than her sister, Yvonne. I watched through the glass as Jason entered the room through another door. He introduced himself and sat down. Roberto's wife fidgeted.

'What is this all about, Officer Abingdon?' she asked, 'And where is my husband?'

'Mrs Altino, it's about the bombing of Renzo Leonardo's car. Your husband ...'

'Is an idiot,' she cut Jason off.

'Sorry?' he asked.

She sat back and folded her arms across her chest.

'Roberto, he's an idiot. What has he told you?'

'Uh ... well ... the truth as you would expect, he's not normally the criminal type ...' Jason faked it.

She shook her head. 'I told him not to get mixed up with Vince; he's bad news. I've been telling my sister that for years, but does she listen? No. She could do so much better.' She was waving her hands now.

Jason nodded, egging her on.

'I shouldn't have told him,' she said to herself.

'Told who, what?' Jason asked.

Mrs Altino looked away. She reddened.

'It's my fault,' she sighed, looking back at Jason. 'I had a one-night stand with Renzo. It was just that,' she added, 'nothing more; Roberto was at a manufacturer's conference. I wish it never happened, and I was consumed with guilt. I love my husband, Officer Abingdon, but ...'

I had stopped listening. I closed my mouth, which seemed to have dropped open in shock. *Roberto's wife had slept with Ren. What was it with that guy? Does he do it whenever it's on offer without thinking of the consequences?* I tuned back in.

'Let me understand this,' Jason summarised. 'You had a one-night stand with Renzo when your husband, Roberto, was away on business?'

Mrs Altino nodded.

'Then, because you were consumed with guilt, you told Roberto?'

She nodded again.

'And he freaked out and ...?'

'He went home to his parents' place, but Yvonne rang and said that she had seen Roberto a few times having coffee with Vince.'

'And why did this surprise you?'

'They weren't close before; Vince was always Renzo's friend,' she said matter-of-factly. 'Roberto agreed with me about Vince. We always thought he was trouble and that Yvonne could do better. We were glad they broke up. See, now he's been hanging around with him, and they have got themselves in trouble.'

Jason nodded.

Keep it going, Jason, I thought. *Start pushing her to tell you how it was done.*

He must have read my mind.

'So, did they do it just to scare him, or did they mean to harm him?' Jason continued to question.

'Oh no,' she answered. 'They were just going to do the anonymous bribery notes for a while. Vince did a good job creating the fake photos of me letting Renzo into our house and the fuzzy long-distance shot of us in bed. The anonymous letter told Renzo he could have the shots if he paid up, otherwise, they would be sent to Roberto.'

My head was spinning. I caught a glance from Jason in my direction. This was out of control. *And Ren! He never, ever mentioned bribery notes to me! Some client!*

Mrs Altino continued. 'You see, Renzo thinks he got away with having a one-night stand with me, and no one was the wiser. But my husband and Vince were gambling on the fact that Renzo would probably do everything in his power to ensure it stayed a secret!'

'But why? If Ren didn't know your husband that well, why would he be worried about him finding out about the affair?' Jason played the devil's advocate.

I hoped Jason wouldn't mention Renzo and Roberto sleeping together.

Mrs Altino stumbled. 'Well, as the old saying goes, "he's soiled in his own nest". He knows Roberto, he knows I'm Yvonne's sister, and at that time, Vince – Ren's best friend – was living with Yvonne.'

Jason wiped his brow. It was doing his head in, too.

'No,' Jason said.

'No?' Mrs Altino looked surprised.

'Yvonne and Vince had broken up when the car was blown up. Would Renzo really care if it came out in the open that he had an affair with you? According to you, he didn't know Roberto that well, so he's not going to care too much about insulting him. He might piss off your sister, but so what? And he wasn't planning on seeing you again, and Yvonne and Vince were over.'

Jason had her. It wasn't enough reason for the bribery. The threat wasn't that Roberto would find out that Ren was sleeping with his wife. The threat was making public that Ren was sleeping with Roberto and Mrs Altino knew it for sure, she was faking.

So, the photos weren't of her and Renzo; they were of Roberto and Renzo.

I sorted through it in my head.

Roberto and Vince anonymously decided to bribe Ren that they would go public with his gay affair. An Italian lover like Ren wouldn't cope with that. Fleecing Ren was obviously enough revenge for all of them.

Jason frowned. He laced his fingers and leaned forward.

'Mrs Altino, we already know the truth. As noble as it is for you to cover for your husband, and illegal, we know he and Renzo were in a relationship and that the bribe was about going public with photos of Roberto and Renzo in a gay affair.'

There it is – all out on the table! Jason was really into the adlibbing now!

'I wouldn't call it a relationship,' she snapped.

Confirmation! She knew!

Jason continued to deliver each point, watching for her reaction. So far, she remained unmoved.

'We know Ren slept with you ... we know Ren slept with your sister ...'

She sat tight-lipped, arms again folded across her chest.

'I understand you want to protect your husband from the public scandal as well ...' Jason finished.

Tears wet her cheeks.

'I don't care about his reputation,' she cleared her throat. 'How will it look to my family? That I can't keep a man? That he has an affair with another man! That I'm not married to a real man?' She reached for her handbag – an expensive Oroton bag – and pulled out a small packet of tissues. She wiped her face.

'I'm sorry,' Jason said. 'What we don't know, and what you can help with, is why blow up the car?' Jason said. 'We know they did it,' he added, 'but why?'

She sighed. 'Because they are idiots.'

Bingo! We had them. We had them for bribery notes that I didn't know existed, for working as a team to get Ren and now for the car as well. I wanted to run in and hug Jason.

'They wanted to show they were serious and that the threat was real. The first letter gave him two days to arrange the cash, but he missed the deadline, so they blew up his car. The second letter said it would be him next time,' she said.

Damn Ren, he hadn't told me any of this.

'How did they do it?' Jason asked.

'They put a bit of ... um, I don't know, some explosive beginning with S, I think, in his car and the detonator in his pager. Vince put it in there when Renzo and Roberto were in the bedroom together,' she shook her head. 'That morning, Renzo and Roberto were supposed to meet for brunch, and it was timed so that Roberto would watch the café from across the street and call Vince when Renzo was out of the car. Vince would then send a message to the pager when Renzo was away from the car and trigger the bomb. But I got called into work ... they are idiots.'

Mrs Altino would be hopeless under torture; she was singing like a canary.

'But when Roberto didn't go to the café ...' Jason prompted her.

'Then Vince didn't have a spotter, so he had to leave enough time to be sure that Renzo would be out of the car and inside the café. He called the pager because it takes a minute or so for the pager service to get the message through; straight after that, he rang Ren to deliver the message that Roberto wasn't coming.

'How much money did you get out of Ren?'

Mrs Altino shrugged. 'None. He asked for more time to raise the money.'

'How much did you ask for?'

'Only one million.'

Jason whistled. 'Where was Ren going to get that money from?'

Mrs Altino made a scoffing sound. 'He could sell some of his luxury cars and manage that easily.'

'Why did they ruffle up the private investigator's boyfriend?'

I froze; that had come out of left field.

'They are such idiots,' she shook her head. 'I didn't know that they went ahead and did that. I knew they were thinking about it because she was getting close to finding out about Roberto and Renzo, and they hadn't got the money yet.'

Jason nodded.

So Dom kept that from me.

'What will happen to Roberto now?' Mrs Altino asked.

Clearly she didn't care about Vince.

'It will depend on whether Ren wants to press charges. Thank you Mrs Altino for cooperating, you have been most generous with your time.'

She nodded, looking exhausted.

'Do you want me to organise a lift home for you?'

'Can I see my husband?' she asked.

'Eventually, if you want to wait, it may be an hour or so. I'll show you through to the waiting room.'

Jason entered the room, and I burst into applause. He laughed.

'Yeah, all in a day's work,' he said.

'That was so exciting,' I told him.

'Amazing how it unfolded,' he agreed. 'You were right about those two, Mr and Mrs Altino; they were too scared to lie.'

'But we don't have written testimony from Mrs Altino. What if Roberto and Vince deny everything?'

Jason shrugged. 'I suspect Roberto won't deny it. I'll go back and read him his rights now, he can get a lawyer, and I'll tell him what we know. As soon as that's official, you can bring Renzo i,n and he can decide if he wants to drop it or press charges.'

'It may be in his best interest to drop it since he's done the wrong thing by all of them,' I said. 'I'll be suggesting that to him.'

'Good,' Jason agreed. 'Will your boyfriend press assault charges?'

'I don't know. I'll ask him. You caught me off guard with that question.'

Jason smiled. 'She's a policeman's dream! I figured she was giving everything else away, worth a shot!'

'Thank you,' I said gratefully. 'I couldn't have got a result without you.'

'It's good for us too. It may only be a small matter on our books, but it is good for our statistics to close it off.'

Ren was horrified.

'Yes!' He slammed his hand on the bar counter. 'Of course I want to press charges. I can't believe it.' He paced up and down, his hands on his hips.

I sat on a barstool at his restaurant, sipped on a diet cola and watched his reaction.

'I mean, these people are supposed to be my friends. What sort of friend would do that? All four of them ...'

He sat on the stool next to me and put his head in his hands. He sighed. 'I want to press charges,' he said again.

I nodded and frowned at him.

'What? You don't think I should?' he asked.

'It's not for me to say, but ...' I started.

'But?'

'Well, it will become a matter of public record and probably will get unwelcome media attention.'

'True,' he said. 'I don't want that.'

'But I think you are being a bit high and mighty, Ren.' I took the gamble of expressing my opinion.

'Go on,' he said.

'You have hurt every one of them. You took Vince's girlfriend; he is your best friend. She had serious feelings for you, and you dumped her after the weekend. You know Roberto is in love with you, yet you flaunt your other relationships in his face and even conquer his wife.' I was worked up. 'These people are supposed to be your friends,' I quoted his own words back to him.

'Fine, then don't press charges since you put it like that,' he folded his arms and glared at me.

'Don't change your mind just because of me,' I said. 'But I think you brought this on yourself and deserve everything you got. Let's face it ... all you lost was your car. If I were one of them, I would have bumped you off when you were inside it!'

He looked shocked. I realised it was time to stop. I stood up and extended my hand.

'Well thanks for the case, Ren, I appreciate the opportunity to have investigated it for you. I hope you are happy at least knowing who did it.' He took my hand and shook it.

I continued. 'I'll let Officer Abingdon know you won't be pressing charges, and I'll send you the final account.'

I was halfway to the door before he stood, and I could hear him following me with long strides. He got to the door before me and opened it for me.

'Thank you, Jesse. I mean it.'

'You're welcome.'

He was smooth, no wonder he charmed everyone. I couldn't wait to invoice him.

Chapter 21

'Case closed! I feel liberated,' I plonked into my office chair and put my feet on the desk. It had been a big day.

'Congratulations! Which case is closed?' Ed put down his pen and looked up at me.

'Ren's case is done and dusted.'

'Who did it?'

'It was a team effort. His best friend and three ex-lovers were in it together,' I gave Ed the details.

'Ren's been busy,' Ed said when I finished. 'We should have champagne to celebrate?'

'Yes! Great idea.'

He went to our office mini bar and pulled out a chilled bottle. While he popped the cork, I rose and grabbed two champagne glasses from the cupboard.

'Are you happy with the result?' Ed asked.

'I am, actually. I'm pleased that no one intended to knock Renzo off. I'm pleased that this is a wake-up call for him. Whether he can mend any bridges with his friends is another matter.' I watched Ed pour. 'He was a shocking client, though ... he never gave me the full story.'

'He wasn't too bright though, was he?' Ed reminded me as he filled our glasses and put the bottle down. He raised his glass. 'To completing your case and getting a result.'

We clinked glasses. 'To results.'

I sipped. 'Nice,' I said. 'Now I've just got to wrap up Jason's case and get onto the choir publicity before Mona begins to hound me.'

⸺ ele ⸺

Jason looked tired. Dark circles edged around his eyes, and he sat slumped in the booth at the coffee shop near his work.

'I've been thinking,' I started. He looked up with raised eyebrows. 'I think, for your sake, we should hurry along and find out if Esme knew about what your father was doing.'

'How?' he asked.

'Remember we spoke about changing your appearance to resemble your father as close as possible? Maybe wear an old suit or a hat the way he wore his hat – something that may make her revert to the past – we could lead the conversation to determine if she knew anything. Would you be willing to try it?'

Jason picked up his spoon and stirred his cappuccino.

'I thought it would come to this, and I am kind of scared of making her think my father's alive. I don't want to hurt her when, or if, she realises he is not.'

'I know. You may need to stay with her until she falls asleep. Perhaps when she wakes, she may not remember that you, or rather, your dad, visited, but there is a risk. Just think about it for a while. It might be our last chance now to find the truth.'

'How are you going with finding my mother's school friends?' he asked.

'No headway,' I reached for my satchel and pulled a manila folder from it. 'I found your mother and her school ...'

'How did you do that? They didn't have the internet when Mom was alive for her to join one of those groups.'

'Sometimes the class president or school reunion organiser will enter all the students' names from that year. That's what has happened here, I imagine, because your mother and about a dozen other students didn't have a profile, just their name listed. The ones with full profiles have obviously joined up and filled them in. Anyway, I found your mom by her birth date. I joined the school reunion club and emailed several of the members. I have had three replies from ladies who remember your mother's name but had nothing to do with her after school.' I read the names to Jason; none were familiar to him.

'I'll let you know if I get any other responses, but I'm not confident.'

He nodded. 'Let's just meet with Esme and get it over with. I'll go through my father's stuff tonight and see what I can find.'

On my way home, Dom called on my phone.

'Congratulations,' he said. 'Ed tells me the case is closed, and Ren's a real tart ... that was Ed's description, not mine.'

'And a fitting one at that,' I said. 'It's over, my love. Why didn't you tell me that Roberto and Vince worked you over?' I thought cutting to the chase rather than ambushing him at home with that one was best.

I heard silence on the other end of the line.

'I didn't know who it was,' he said hesitantly. 'It's like I told you, two guys in the car park ambushed me. I wouldn't know Vince and Rob ...?'

'Roberto,' I finished.

'Right, Roberto, I wouldn't know them if I fell over them.'

'But when they told you to tell me to drop the case, you would have made the connection,' I continued.

I heard Dom sigh. 'Fine, detective, I didn't tell you because I didn't want to freak you out. I wanted to persuade you to give up this PI stuff without saying 'see, look what's happened, told you so'.'

'You could have told Jason when he dropped in to speak with you.'

'Yeah, I meant to thank you for that. Looks great having a cop drop in to see you at your place of work.'

I was antagonising him, which was getting us nowhere.

'I'm sorry, Dom. I hate the thought that you were beaten up because of me. I don't want to give up my work, but I promise to choose less dangerous cases.'

'Really?' Dom sounded happy.

'I'll do my best,' I assured him.

Chapter 22

JASON CALLED ME TWO days later. He was incoherent on the phone, but eventually, I was able to ascertain that, on a whim, he had taken on his father's persona and been to see Esme. What he heard confused him more, and he wanted me to give him my opinion. We agreed to meet in an hour, and I could sense his agitation when I pushed open the café door. He alternated between wringing his hands and stirring his coffee too much.

He looked relieved to see me.

'I've ordered for you, I hope that's OK? Thanks for meeting me ...'

'Thank you, that's fine. Are you alright?'

'I don't know.'

'Start at the beginning,' I instructed.

Jason placed his hands on the table in front of him and exhaled. 'This is what happened ...' he began.

The morning got off to a promising start. He had arrived at the aged-care home, dressed in his father's suit and shirt, feeling like he was going to a bad seventies party.

Esme was in her room. She sat in her chair clutching a pale blue wool wrap around her shoulders. As he approached, she looked up and clapped her hands with delight upon seeing him.

'Charles,' she exclaimed.

Jason's heart started racing. There was no going back now. He sat beside her and took her hands in his. They sat this way for several minutes.

'Where are my manners? I'll make tea,' Esme clutched the arms of the chair to lift herself.

'Allow me,' Jason said.

After doing so, he sat down beside her, and they drank from the fine china cups. She put her hands in her lap, turned them back and forth and sighed.

'What is it, Esme?' Jason asked, balancing his cup of tea on his knee.

'My hands,' she stared at them. 'They were beautiful once. Do you remember?'

'I remember,' Jason smiled at her. 'I still think they are beautiful.'

'Oh, Charles,' she looked at him and back at her hands. 'I used to take great care of my hands, but there's no stopping aging.'

'We've grown old together, isn't that wonderful?' he continued to prod.

'*Grow old along with me, the best is yet to be,*' Esme sighed again. 'That's from a poem.'

'I know,' Jason said.

'Do you remember it? I wrote it to you ... the day before our wedding.'

'How could I forget?' Jason lied. 'We've had a wonderful life together; I am a lucky man.' He removed his father's tweed jacket, which revealed a pale blue shirt with an enormous collar.

'I was worried,' she said.

'Why?'

'I was worried it came at too great a price for you.'

'What do you mean?'

'My sister ...' Esme stopped speaking.

Jason waited, not wanting to interrupt. Eventually, he spoke. 'I always loved you, my dear Emmy,' he whispered.

Esme smiled and looked up at him. 'You haven't called me that for the longest time.'

'You thought I had forgotten?'

'Yes,' she nodded.

'How could I forget?'

Esme sighed. 'Bella and Emmy; that is what you called us both. Poor, poor, Bella.'

'What happened to Isabella was out of our hands,' Jason continued.

Esme nodded. 'We don't get to choose who lives or dies … but … maybe I could have saved her.'

'How could you have saved her, my dear? She was ill. She would have wanted us to be together, to bring up Jason as a family,' he continued. He followed her gaze as she looked out the window.

'Do you think she will forgive me … in the afterlife?' Esme asked as she continued to look at the garden. 'I worry about that sometimes. Isabella will be in heaven, but will I?'

Jason ran his tongue over his lips; his mouth was dry. He continued.

'What is there to forgive you for?'

Esme shrugged. 'They say confession is good for the soul …' she continued.

'Did you want to confess … did you want a priest?' Jason offered.

'Oh Charles, I did that long ago,' Esme sighed. Then she sat up straight. 'Charles, do you remember my timber box? The one with the roses painted on the front?'

Panic welled from the pit of Jason's stomach. *Box, what box? I don't remember reading anything about a box in any of the letters.*

'Well ...' he exhaled.

She wrung her hands. 'I should have destroyed it. I wanted to destroy it years ago. I have to do that, Charles!' she turned to him, tears in her eyes. 'Can you do that for me without looking inside? Can you?'

'Emmy, I have a confession to make,' Jason put his teacup on the table and took her hands again. 'Don't be frightened,' he noticed her stricken look, 'it's a silly confession; I can't remember where the box is.'

Esme smiled and then giggled in a girlish fashion. 'Charles, you are getting old! It was in the bedroom cupboard underneath the floor panel. Remember? I had my diary in there, and you promised not to read it.'

Jason threw his head back and laughed. 'Yes! You are right, and I am getting old.' He rubbed her hands. 'I'll get rid of it. I'll do it today.'

'Yes, good, get rid of it,' she looked outside again, 'that's the best idea.'

Jason's eyes seemed to refocus, and he saw me opposite him.

'What do you think?' he asked.

'I think you need to find that box, and we need to find the priest that Esme confessed to if he is still alive.'

Chapter 23

I met Melanie for cocktail hour; she looked great in a red wool dress with black boots.

Saturday afternoon at the bar was popular. A four-piece jazz band was playing, and we managed to score a seat not too close to the band so we could hear ourselves speak.

'We have to find another bar,' Melanie looked around.

'Why?' I grabbed the wine list and scanned it for a dry sparkling by the glass.

Melanie lowered her voice. 'Don't you think this place is getting older?'

I looked around. 'It only opened a few months ago.'

'No. Older clientele. Look at some of the people here. I don't want to be in the mutton dressed up as lamb crowd.'

I looked at Melanie and shook my head.

'What?' she was defensive. 'I'm probably just saying what everyone's thinking!'

'Never occurred to me,' I said and caught the waiter's attention. 'But I don't care where we go. So if you want to find a bar full of lambs, fine by me.'

She smiled as though I had endorsed her strange thoughts. The waiter arrived, and I ordered a glass of sparkling wine, and Melanie ordered a Manhattan.

'Now listen,' Melanie glared at me. 'I have to tell you something that you can't tell anyone else. It has to go in the Mel and Jesse secret vault!'

'Mel!'

'What?' she looked startled.

'That's it!' I just realised something I had overlooked.

'What?'

'Esme. My client's aunty must have had a best friend. I asked Jason if his mother had a close friend, but I forgot about Esme! Who could commit a crime and not tell someone? Everyone talks.'

'Right,' Melanie was catching on. 'I guess so.'

'Especially women; look at the two of us. There's not one secret we haven't shared, is there?'

Melanie thought about it. 'No, you know pretty much everything.'

'Exactly. And you are the only person who knows everything about me. I've told you things I haven't even told my mother. So Esme must have a best friend somewhere who will know her secrets.'

'If they're worth knowing,' Melanie shrugged, unfamiliar with my case.

'They're worth knowing,' I smiled, 'and assuming the friend is still alive, this could be big.'

Our drinks arrived, and we toasted good luck and good shopping.

'So back to me ... this is for the secret vault,' Melanie continued while a thousand thoughts ran through my head.

—ele—

Jason and I talked over each other on the phone.

'I've found the priest,' he exclaimed.

'Has she got a best friend?' I asked.

'What? The priest?'

'What? No, Esme, a best friend? Sorry. Let's start again,' I suggested. 'You found the priest that heard Esme's confession?'

'Yes, he's alive, but he won't tell me anything,' Jason moaned.

'Well, that sucks,' I said. 'Surel,y after all this time ...'

'I tried that. I also tried the sympathy bid with the poor, conscience-ridden son argument, the need to make peace to move on, blah, blah, blah. Nothing worked. He said he could never pass on a confession that was told in confidence.'

I thought about it. 'I guess there's no way we could trick him out of it?'

'You're going straight to hell,' Jason teased. 'No. He may be old, but he's as sharp as a tack, and I wouldn't be surprised if he remembers the confession word for word.'

'That's too frustrating,' I said. 'What about the box?'

'It's not where Esme said it was. The floorboard was loose, but nothing was there. I searched the whole room. I'm so frustrated I could just ...'

'Kill someone?' I suggested.

'Throw it in,' he offered.

I gave Jason my "best friend" theory.

'Makes sense,' he said. 'Let me think.'

'It's not the lady who lived next door ... you know, she called me by her name by mistake?'

'No, that was Merle ... it wasn't her,' Jason said, still in thought. 'Esme had several close friends, and they did everything in a group. For years, they used to meet for high tea on the first Saturday of the month. I remember her getting dressed up to go. I can't remember their names now; it's been too long, but they worked with her.'

'Well, that helps; I can track it from there. Where did she work?'

Jason dropped a bomb on me. 'She was a nurse at the General Hospital.'

∼∼∼

I am such an idiot. I berated myself all through my jog with Atlas.

Why didn't I ask if and where Esme worked? It was not the 1940s when this took place; it was the 1970s! Women did have jobs and careers then! And she's a nurse! She had access to any number of medicines and techniques that could have shortened her sister's life, maybe without Charles even knowing or maybe with his help.

I had to find that box. The chances are that if she was involved at all, then that's where the evidence lies.

Chapter 24

ALICE COLE WAS A fiery old girl. I couldn't imagine her among the dainty setting of a high tea with the ladies, but I could imagine her being matron in the hospital ward.

'Esme,' she exclaimed, 'she was great fun, our Essie. Charles, on the other hand, was dull, dull, dull. I never knew what she saw in him. I've seen Esme a few times since she went into the home, but she's deteriorated,' she stopped and looked me up and down as we stood in her kitchen making coffee.

'There's some debate as to whether it's hereditary, you know?'

'Dementia? Alzheimers?' I asked.

'Hereditary,' she repeated. 'Yes, I still subscribe to the medical journals even though I'm retired. Fascinating reading. The current thought is that if your parents get it after age 65, then there's no obvious inheritance pattern.'

'Well, that's comforting, I guess,' I said. 'But I'm not related to Esme.'

'Oh, well, you must look at your family history then.'

I followed Alice into the lounge room, where she carried a tray laden with a pot of coffee, cups, and an apple tea cake. She put the tray on the table, and we sat on the couch.

'Will you have some apple tea cake? I made it this morning.'

'Ye,s please.' Who would turn down homemade apple tea cake?

'Are you married?' she blurted out. Alice would make a good private investigator; I may have to recruit her.

'No.'

'Don't leave it too long,' she advised. 'I know your generation keeps putting it off, but you want to be thinking about children. The pill was the best thing that happened in my time.'

She raised an eyebrow in my direction. I wasn't sure I wanted her to continue along that train of thought.

'Can you imagine how it liberated women? We no longer had to marry men to have a family and weren't slaves to the breeding routine, so we could work and have our own lives. Of course that works both ways,' she offered me the sugar. 'Men now don't need to marry women for sex and therefore can avoid doing so for as long as they want to play the field.'

I was pretty confident Alice would not be short of an opinion.

'All true,' I agreed. I put my cup and saucer back on the table. 'Would you say you were Esme's best friend in the group?'

'Oh no, dear, but we were close. We all did our nursing training together. That was in the days when it was done in the hospitals, not in the universities like it is now. Ridiculous,' she shook her head.

I didn't want to ask, but I had to.

'Why do you say that?'

'Well, the skills shortage, my dear. When the nurses were trained in the hospitals, they had all hands on deck for three years while learning on the job. They started at the bottom and gained skills as they went along. Now they go to college, the hospitals are desperately short of nurses, and they all graduate thinking they are too good to empty a bedpan!'

I nodded. I wanted to get back to Esme.

'So, who was in your group?'

'There was Esme, myself, Diane and Marianna.'

None of the names sounded familiar, and Esme had not mentioned them during my couple of visits.

'Do you still see them regularly?' I prodded.

'For a long time, we met monthly, but we stopped doing so a few years ago,' she refilled our cups from the pot. 'Then Esme went into the home, so we started meeting monthly in her room, but it wasn't long before she didn't recognise us, so we stopped doing that. It was distressing as well. Then Diane was killed in a car accident.'

'Oh, I'm sorry,' I said, surprised.

'Yes, an awful thing. She was driving home from the theatre and a drunk driver hit her. They say it was instant. We always wondered who would be the first to go in our group.'

'I wonder if Diane is luckier than Esme?' I thought aloud.

'I've wondered that same thing myself, Jesse, many times. And I suspect Diane is luckier, although no one got a chance to say goodbye.'

I nodded. 'And Marianna?'

'Marianna and I still catch up occasionally for lunch,' Alice said. 'Marianna is a gentle soul. I suspect I am too strong-willed for her. Now, she is the one who was closest to Esme,' Alice said with emphasis. 'Thick as thieves the two of them were. There's nothing they wouldn't do for each other. They even asked to work the same shifts together.'

I was still processing everything Alice had told me, so much so that Dominic had been talking to me for several minutes, and I missed it completely.

'So, is that a yes?' he asked.

I turned to look at him walking beside me. Atlas was stopping regularly to sniff and pee.

'You didn't hear a word I said, did you?' he grinned.

'Is this role reversal?' I asked. 'You're the guy; you're not supposed to listen to me.'

'I try my best to uphold that,' he teased.

'Sorry,' I slipped my hand into his and held Atlas's lead with the other.

'That's OK,' he said. 'I wasn't discussing the meaning of life or anything. I just asked you to marry me.'

'What?' I stopped dead.

Dominic continued to smile at me.

'Will you marry me?' he asked.

'Now?' It's all I could think of to say.

Dominic looked around. 'Do you see a priest in the shrubbery?'

I laughed and pulled in closer to him. 'Didn't we discuss this last month, before you moved in? I thought the moving-in exercise was supposed to cement the relationship. What brought this on?'

Dom pointed to an elderly couple sitting on a timber bench on the banks of the lake, feeding the ducks. I watched as he pulled the bread apart, and she threw it into the water. They looked so content.

'I know you don't want to marry,' Dom continued to watch them, 'but I do. So now and then, when I see something romantic, I'm going to propose. One day, you may say yes. But if you decide to make it official, try not to leave it until we're that old. I want to look fit and reasonably good in the wedding photos.'

I looked up at him and smiled. 'I may surprise you and ask you one day.'

'Then the answer will definitely be 'no',' he teased.

'How much were you planning on spending on the ring?'

Dominic grinned and shrugged. 'Just a couple of thousand, I guess.'

I nodded. 'I'll give it some thought.'

Marianna was the complete opposite of Alice. She was small and sophisticated. She came from money, and nearly every finger was adorned with diamonds.

'It's heartbreaking for me seeing Esme like that,' she said as we met for high tea.

'I can imagine it would be,' I selected a small pastry from the top plate of the high tea display. It was Marianna's idea to have a high tea since we were talking about Esme. Neither Marianna nor Alice seemed to care who I was or that I was investigating Esme, not that I told them as much. Perhaps they were just happy to have the company and talk about the past.

'Does she still recognise you?' I asked.

'Most times, yes,' Marianna continued. 'Most people with Alzheimer's or Dementia remember the past more vividly than they remember the most recent events in their life.'

'Odd, isn't it?' I sipped my tea and looked around. It was a lovely environment. The room was filled with large pots of flowers, and the waiters wore crisp black and white. I imagine doing this regularly would have been fun for the ladies.

'Who is your best friend dear?' Marianna asked me.

I told her about Melanie, and she laughed at some of my descriptions.

'We've known each other for nearly ten years,' I finished.

'It's lovely to have friends you grow with,' Marianna agreed. 'Esme and I met when we started nursing, so we go back decades.'

'I want to talk to you about the death of Esme's sister, Isabella,' I watched her face for a reaction. She looked surprised at the mention of the name, and then something appeared to shut down. I decided to take a gamble.

'I'm a friend of Isabella's son and Esme's nephew, Jason ...'

She nodded. 'I remember Jason.'

I trod carefully.

'Jason loves Esme, but he has always felt that he didn't do enough for his mother in her dying weeks.'

'He was only a little boy,' she interrupted.

'Yes,' I agreed. 'But she said something to him that now, as an adult, he wonders if he should have told someone or if it was true.'

Marianna didn't interrupt me.

'His mother told him that she was being poisoned and to get help.'

Marianna didn't move or express any shock. *Very strange.*

'You can imagine now, as an adult, how that worries him. He thought maybe ... maybe his father knew his mother was dying and, with his pharmaceutical background, helped release her earlier,' I chose my words.

'Or maybe Esme – who also had access to hospital stocks – did the same?' Marianna read my mind.

'Maybe she did, to help her sister ...' I concurred, not implying there would be any other motive. I let her question hang for a little while before I spoke again.

'We know Charles was in love with Esme. We found the love letters.' I stopped then and played the silent card to see what would happen.

Marianna continued to eat a small sandwich in a very ladylike manner. She finished, wiped her mouth and hands on a napkin, took a sip of tea and looked around. I wasn't sure if she would leave, ignore me or share some knowledge with me.

'And what would Jason do if he discovered the truth now?' Marianna asked.

'Nothing,' I assured her. 'It's for his peace of mind. If nothing happened, then he can be reassured by that. If it did, then his mother didn't die in vain; he knew what happened.'

Marianna didn't say anything. She was using my tactics.

'What could he do?' I continued. 'Charles is long gone.'

'And Esme?' she asked.

'It would be one person's word against another, and Jason would never harm Esme or take it any further. Besides, what judge in the country would send her to jail?' I had overstepped my mark. I hadn't suggested that Esme was involved or responsible before, but it was too late now.

'What were you hoping to find from talking to me, dear?' Marianna questioned in a steady voice.

'Girlfriends talk; they rely on each other. I hoped maybe Esme confided in you or maybe ... she mentioned a box, a timber one with roses ... maybe you know where it is?'

Marianna reached for her handbag. 'Please don't be offended when I say this, but I don't wish to say anything further to you about Esme. But I would like to meet with you and Jason. Perhaps then, we can continue this.'

Chapter 25

I HAD BEEN OUT of the office for a day, working on Jason's case. Ed clapped when he saw me.

'Welcome back,' he teased, 'I was just about to take your name off the door!'

'Hello! My name's not on the door,' I reminded him.

'Well, that saves me removing it, another job off my list.'

I placed a cappuccino from the downstairs deli in front of him.

'Hmm, good coffee,' he inhaled the aroma. 'So how have you been, Ms PI, and what's been happening?'

I gave him a full rundown of my activities. When I finished, he threw his empty coffee cup in the bin.

'That's better than television!'

I laughed. 'Thanks. One day away from the office feels like forever. Did I miss much today?'

It was Ed's turn to give me a rundown of events. Then I started to wade through the seventy-two emails and several messages on my desk.

'Don't let all those emails get to you,' Ed sensed my mood. 'I've got a great idea. It's 10am now. Let's do a two-hour blitz on PR work – no talking and no private phone calls, only work calls – and then at 12 sharp, let's go to the bar for lunch.'

The challenge perked me up. 'You're on, great idea!'

'Starting now!' Ed declared.

I had to restrain myself not to call Jason, but it was Ed's two-hour PR blitz, and I had to abide by the rules of the game. I would see Jason this evening anyway. We were meeting with Marianna at her home at 6pm.

If she tells him the truth, the case will be wrapped up, and I can send an invoice, which is the best part of any job! OK, second best to getting paid. Speaking of which, I logged onto my banking page, and it was there! Renzo had paid his bill. Lovely.

I messaged Dominic to remind him I would be home after 8pm and to feel free to cook a great dinner in readiness for my arrival. It pays to be optimistic. I drove through the leafy suburb where Marianna lived. I picked her for having money, and her house said it all: a huge Georgian mansion with a long driveway that arched around the house in a loop. The gate automatically opened before I pressed the buzzer; I drove in. Jason's car was there, and he was standing on the front steps with Marianna. He must have just arrived.

I greeted them, and Jason and I exchanged looks as we followed her into what she called the sitting room. I call it a waste of room; some houses have unused rooms for all occasions.

We declined tea and coffee. I could tell Jason was nervous. He was torn – wanting to hear but not wanting to know what Marianna said.

I observed Marianna sizing up Jason. She may not have told him anything if he had not been a gentleman. She seemed to like him.

'I met your mother,' she said. 'She came to the theatre with Esme and me several times. She was lovely, but they were quite different as sisters.'

Jason nodded. 'I never knew my mother that well. I was fairly young when she died, and it was only in the last few months of my mother's life that Esme moved in, and I saw them together as sisters.'

'Of course,' Marianna said. 'They both loved your father, though.'

'Yes,' Jason agreed. 'Some of our family friends told me that my father took Mom's death hard. But I also found the love letters between Esme and my father, so I know they truly loved each other … even when my mother was still alive,' he added with a bitter voice.

I nudged him under the table. I wanted him to look like the victim who needed to put the past behind him, not a bitter son out to get his aunty.

Marianna continued, 'I imagine Esme's love was a great source of comfort to your father during the last few months of your mother's life. Sometimes, that brings people together and gets them through adversity.'

Jason looked like he was taking her comments on board. 'Yes,' he finally said. 'I never thought of it like that.'

'I have something I would like to give you,' she rose, and so did we. 'No please, make yourselves comfortable, I'll just be a minute.'

We watched her walk from the room, and Jason turned to me.

'Sorry,' he whispered.

I shrugged. 'No need to be. This is not textbook stuff; it's real life. You have a right to be upset.'

'I feel like getting in the car and speeding away from here,' he ran his hands over his face.

'You've come this far,' I reminded him, 'this could be the last hurdle.'

Chapter 26

I saw Jason the next day. He was relieved. He offered me Esme's small timber box with the faded roses painted on the front, the box that Marianna had given him. In it were all the answers he needed. He looked less tortured as he told me all the secrets it revealed. When he finished, I shook my head. 'I didn't think she would do it, give away her best friend's secrets.'

'The secrets of a lifetime,' Jason agreed. 'Well, she didn't really. She never said anything to confirm it; she just handed over the box, but the contents said it all.'

'The vault of friendship,' I thought aloud.

'What's that?' Jason asked.

'Oh, nothing. So has knowing brought you any closure?'

'I'm relieved, Jesse, and sad too.'

'I know,' I reached for his hand, 'I understand that.'

'Thank you. I couldn't have put this to rest if it hadn't been for you.'

'I think you could have,' I smiled at him, 'but maybe you just needed someone not as emotionally involved to take the journey with you.'

'Will you send the bill to my email address?'

'Of course,' I agreed.

'I'll miss our coffees,' he said and looked away.

'Don't think you're getting off the coffee hook,' I teased him. 'You're my only inside police contact. I need your help. The only difference will be that I'm paying for the coffee.'

Jason laughed and slid from the booth. I joined him, and we held each other in a quick hug. He picked up the box.

'Are you sure you don't want to read through it for yourself for your closure?' he asked.

'No, but thanks. Your peace of mind is the only closure I'm seeking.'

He headed for the door and looked back at me. With a quick nod, he was gone, and the case was closed.

Dominic sat with me on our front step as we watched the dusk parade of people pass by on the footpath. He topped up my red wine.

'So finish the story for me?' he said. 'What was in Esme's box?'

'Enough to close the case,' I said.

'Really?' Dom looked pleased. 'Congratulations.'

'Thanks. Marianna wouldn't tell us anything. She was loyal to the end.'

'You have to admire that,' he said.

'I do,' I agreed. 'But she had the box that Esme wanted to be destroyed. I don't know why she didn't destroy it or decide to give it to us. Maybe she always felt guilty by association, and this way, she absolves herself by giving Jason his closure.'

'What was in there?'

'Jason told me that all the test results were in there – pages and pages of results kept by Esme on her patient, Isabella – she had used the experiment that Charles found.'

'The sugar, rats and immune system one?'

'Yes. Charles must have been trying it on rats in his lab, and Esme found it and tried it on her sister. She's written it in her diary – the daily doses, Isabella's heart rate, the weight loss – it's all unbearably sad. She also writes about her anguish at seeing Charles trying desperately to save Isabella with all these radical ideas and treatments. She wrote that at one stage, Charles was attempting to reverse the immune experiment to strengthen Isabella's immune system while she, Esme, was trying to weaken it. '

'So while Charles was trying to save Isabella, Esme was killing her,' Dom summarised.

'Precisely.'

'Do you think Charles ever found out about Esme's involvement?'

'I don't think so,' I said. 'When Esme thought Jason was Charles, she was still talking in riddles, saying she could have saved Isabella but not saying she was responsible for her death. She asked him to destroy the box and her diary without looking through them. I imagine the priest heard the truth, though.'

Dom sighed. 'Jason must feel like the world's lifted off his shoulders to know that his father loved and wanted to save his mother.'

'It's a huge relief for him,' I agreed. 'But terribly sad to think he could have grown up with a mother if it wasn't for Esme.'

'Seems unfair she got away with it,' Dom said. 'If I were Jason, I would still want to confront her, no matter how old she is now.'

'I feel the same,' I agreed. 'After all, this was well planned; Esme ran the experiment for nearly three months, recording every detail of Isabella's deteriorating health.'

'How could you do it to your sister?' Dom shook his head.

'I asked Jason the same question. He said that if you read the diary, you would see a long history of jealousy. Isabella won the awards; everyone thought Isabella was beautiful, sweet, and funny, and on it goes. Esme writes that she had a crush on

Charles first, and then he met Isabella. I think the sisterly love was one-sided.'

'So what is Jason going to do now?'

'Nothing,' I told Dom. 'Esme hasn't long left in this world, and she has no memory of what's happening most of the time.'

'Well ... that's it,' Dom said, 'two different cases, two cases closed.'

We sat in silence for a while. A young couple went past with their dog on the lead, and Atlas ensured they knew this was his territory.

Dom reached over and took my hand. 'I love you,' he said.

'I love you too,' I replied. 'And you can be sure I'll never poison you to run off with your brother.'

'I don't have a brother.'

'Must make you feel safer then,' I said.

'Marry me?' he smiled.

'You're killing me.'

'Yes. I'm breaking down your immunity to marriage.'

'How much were you planning to spend on the ring?'

Dominic grinned and shrugged. 'Just a couple of thousand, I guess.'

I nodded. 'I'll give it some thought.'

THE END

From the author

BEING A JOURNALIST AT heart, it was great fun researching and writing this cosy mystery, just as it was for *Death by Disguise* and *Death by Reunion*.

Should you wish to explore more, I have used elements of truth in all the books – the science experiment in *Death by Sugar*; the techniques of mask making and the very sad story of the Mexican bride in *Death by Disguise*; and the Titanic Mourning Bears and Australian victims in *Death by Reunion*.

Thank you for reading Jesse's story. I hope you enjoyed yourself, and I look forward to crossing paths with you next time Jesse and Dominic venture out.

My sincere thanks to:

- Karri, Art by Karri, for the wonderful cover design;

- Ro Parkinson, Michael Congreve and Merle Goltz for proofreading and feedback;

- And most importantly, Atlas B. Goltz, who lives on in Jesse's tales and my heart forever.

DEATH BY REUNION:

It is 10 years since Jesse Clarke finished high school, and it is time to celebrate with a reunion. There are a few shocks – and that doesn't include Jesse running a publicity and a private investigator business – rather, the talk of the reunion is Alex Bryson, the overweight kid who transformed himself into a handsome, fit pilot. But a week after the reunion, Alex is found dead.

That's not the only reunion that's taking up Jesse's time. At a family reunion and 80th birthday celebration for a family matriarch, a very expensive Titanic relic goes missing –a Titanic Mourning Bear who just happens to be appearing in photographs all around the country!

Jesse has her work cut out in both cases. With support above and beyond the call of duty from her boyfriend, Dominic, along with her grumpy and reliable business partner Ed, Police Officer Jason, and Jesse's enthusiastic best friend, Melanie, Jesse is back solving mysteries while juggling publicity clients including Mona and her choir, again.

Also by Helen Goltz

MISS HAYWARD & THE Detective Series (historical mystery/romance):
Murder at the Carnival
The Artist's Missing Muse
Mystery at the Asylum
The Mortician's Clue
Murder in Bridal Lane

The Lady Mortician's Visions (historical mystery/romance/paranormal twist)
The Missing Brides
The Fake Child
The Dastardly Debutante
The Deathly Dolls
The Potent Perfume
The Watery Grave
More to come....

The Clairvoyant's Glasses (supernatural/urban fantasy romance)

Volume 1 – A vision unexpected

Volume 2 – Time has a shadow

Volume 3 – Love knows no bounds

Volume 4 – Fate comes to call

The Mitchell Parker series published by *Next Chapter* (crime thrillers):

Mastermind

Graveyard of the Atlantic

The Fourth Reich

Writing as Jack Adams (psychological mystery/suspense):

Poster Girl

Delaney and Murphy childhood friends series:

Asylum

Stalker

Cult

Hitched

Carnival.

The Jesse Clarke series (contemporary mysteries):

Death by Sugar

Death by Disguise

Death by Reunion

Writing with journalist Chris Adams, *The Grave Tales* series (non-fiction) x 9 titles:

Grave Tales: Brisbane Vol.1

Grave Tales: Great Ocean Road – Geelong to Port Fairy

Grave Tales: Sydney Vol.1

Grave Tales: Bruce Highway

Grave Tales: True Crime Vol.1

Grave Tales: Queensland's Great South West

Grave Tales: Melbourne Vol.1

Grave Tales: Queensland's Scenic Rim & Surrounds

Grave Tales: Tasmania.

Grave Tales: Cold Cases (an amalgamation of stories from existing titles)

Writing as Ally Adams:

The Saints team (contemporary romance):

Team Lucas

Team Tomas

Team Niklas

Team Alex

Stand-alone titles:

The House on Findlater Lane (mystery/romance paranormal)

The Forgotten House (historical romance)

Three Parts Truth (mystery suspense)

Morphers (middle grade fiction).

About the author

Helen is a hybrid-published, Amazon best-selling author. After studying English Literature, Media, and Communications at universities in Queensland, Australia, and obtaining a Counselling Diploma, Helen has worked as a journalist, producer and marketer in print, TV, radio and public relations. Born in Toowoomba, she has made her home in Logan Village, Australia, with her journalist husband, Chris, and Boxer dog, Baxter. She is published by Next Chapter and her own imprint, Atlas Productions.

Connect with Helen:

Website: www.helengoltz.com

BookBub:www.bookbub.com/authors/helen-goltz

Facebook: www.facebook.com/HelenGoltz.Author

Instagram: https://www.instagram.com/helengoltz1/

9 780980 753219